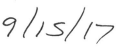

9/15/17

Teach Me:
Brie's Submission

By
Red Phoenix

I hope you enjoy
Brie's journey again
and again.

Red Phoenix

Teach Me: Brie's Submission

Copyright © 2016 by Red Phoenix
Print Edition

RedPhoenix69@live.com

Edited by Amy Parker, Proofed by Marilyn Cooper
Cover by CopperLynn
Phoenix symbol by Nicole Delfs

Adult Reading Material (18+)

Dedication

Tons of love and kisses to my husband, affectionately known as MrRed.

Not only is he my everything, but he continues to be my biggest supporter.

You make my life beautiful, my love!

To my awesome fans who have become like family.

CONTENTS

The Invitation

B rianna put the money in the register and slammed it closed. It was another dull day in the tiny tobacco shop. This was so *not* what she wanted for her life. She had gone to college and studied for four long years to get her degree in film, only to find that it would open no doors for her here in Hollywood. It was all about who you knew or who your daddy was. Four years and thousands in debt—and for what? To work full-time in this little tobacco shop day after day, making her home-made movies on the weekends and hoping for a break? *Pathetic.*

She adjusted her ponytail. It was one of those morn-ings when her curly brown hair refused to cooperate. Luckily for Brie, she looked good in a ponytail. Well, at least that was what she told herself.

"Brie, don't forget to put out the new cigarettes. Sev-eral people complained about having to wait while we searched for their brand," Mr. Reynolds called out from the back of the shop.

It was technically Jeff's job, but the lazy shit never

did anything. All the grunt work fell on Brie's shoulders because she was reliable. What a horrible thing to be. Being labeled as 'the reliable one' meant that she was stuck doing everyone else's job. Brie didn't hold it against her boss, Mr. Reynolds, though. He wasn't responsible for hiring the staff. The owner did that, and he mainly hired people within his family (which Brie was not). To his credit, Mr. Reynolds gave her a nice raise every time her evaluation came up. Still, she always got stuck taking up the slack, and it wasn't fair. *Not in the least!*

Brie bent down and began opening the boxes to shelve the cigarettes. The sound of a man clearing his throat caused her to look up.

She was startled to see a strikingly handsome couple standing before her. The woman had long, red hair and the most tight-fitting leather outfit Brie had ever seen. Somehow, the lady didn't look cheap in the hot little outfit. No, this woman oozed confidence and sex appeal. Very classy.

The man, however, made her tremble a little. His intense gaze seemed to go right through Brie. He was tall and incredibly attractive, with short, brown hair and chiseled facial features. However, it was those eyes that commanded her attention.

"Miss, could I have a pack of Treasurer Aluminium Black Cigarettes?"

Brie smiled apologetically. She knew they were some of the most expensive cigarettes made. "I'm sorry. We don't carry those here." The cigarettes were over fifty bucks a pack and the little tobacco shop did not serve that type of clientele.

The gentleman looked around and nodded. "Satisfy my curiosity and tell me what brand is in the box over there."

He pointed to a box just out of her reach. Brie bent down and opened it up. She chuckled when she saw what was inside. "Sorry, these are just Marlboro Lights." She stood up and turned to face him. Brie caught him staring at her butt and blanched. No one ever looked at her that way. It was embarrassing. Well, somewhat embarrassing. Okay, it was kind of cool…but how dare he?!

The man raised an eyebrow and smiled slightly. It was exhilarating.

"Do you have any Fantasia Cigarettes?" the stunning redhead asked.

Brie grinned. "Now *those* we do carry." She stood on tiptoe to get a pack off the top shelf and handed it to the woman. "Is that all?"

"Do you like it here?" the man asked in a low, alluring voice that sent chills through her.

Why was he asking?

"Not exactly," she answered, but her heart started racing at the thought that this might be her lucky break. The gentleman could be some big-time producer who wanted to give this little tobacco shopkeeper a chance.

"I'm not surprised. You don't look as if you belong here." The man put a hundred-dollar bill on the counter.

"I'm sorry; I don't have change for that."

He shrugged. "No matter. I don't need the change."

The man lightly stroked the length of his girlfriend's

arm. It looked so sensual and loving. Brie wished a guy would touch her like that. He caught her staring at them. She quickly glanced away, berating herself. *How pitiful am I?*

The redhead picked up the cigarettes gracefully and slipped them in her purse. She took her lover's arm and smiled up at him. "Thank you, Sir."

Brie thought it a little odd that the woman had called him 'sir', but the man kissed her hand tenderly. "I'm sure we can find a way for you to repay me." They walked out of the store without looking back.

Brie watched them leave, wishing she could trade places with that woman. She looked down at the counter and saw Benjamin Franklin staring up at her. Her heart raced again. Would it be okay to pocket it when the man had obviously wanted her to have it? She rang in the price of the cigarettes and hesitated before picking it up.

Underneath the bill was a business card. Brie took a closer look and read:

> *The Submissive Training Center*
> *25 Years of Excellence*

She looked down at the bottom and saw a phone number and website address. Brie wondered if the gentleman had accidentally left it behind, so she stuffed it in her pocket just in case he returned. Brie stared hard at the money before she put it in the till, deciding to talk to Mr. Reynolds about it. The change from a hundred-dollar bill was *not* worth her reputation.

When she got home after work that night, Brie

fished out the business card. Out of curiosity, she typed the web address into her tablet. The screen that popped up looked exceedingly professional. The organization appeared to be a community college of some sort. She pressed the information link and her jaw dropped.

The pictures at the top of the screen showed women in various B&D poses. One girl had her hands tied behind her back, and she was kneeling before a man dressed in leather. Another girl was facing the camera, but Brie could just see the swell of her naked ass. The guy behind her was holding an unusual whip and looked as if he were about to take a swing.

Brie quickly exited the site, shocked by what she'd seen. Why would the man carry around a business card like that and why would he give it to *her*? She shivered when she thought of him checking out her butt and was extremely glad she hadn't kept his money.

She went to bed with those images still etched in her mind. Although she was tired, she couldn't sleep. Eventually, curiosity got the better of her and Brie grabbed her tablet, bringing it to her bed. She revisited the site, wanting to check out the rest of the pictures. Even though she found them shocking, seeing the girls in those various poses was exceedingly hot.

There was one position in particular that Brie found intriguing. The girl's wrists and ankles were bound to a table. She was dressed in an outfit that barely covered her most intimate parts. Her legs were spread wide open, and there was the hint of another person just out of reach of the camera. What struck Brie was the look on the girl's face. She was looking at the unseen person with

5

an expression of anticipation and lust. For whatever reason, that picture really turned her on.

She looked through all of the information on the website. Apparently, people could take a six-week 'course' and learn how to become a skilled submissive. It seemed such a strange thing to study, and she wondered what possible benefit there was to becoming proficient at something like that.

Brie found a link to reviews of the program and read, 'My life has changed since taking the course. I have found my true calling and have never felt more alive.'

She figured the woman must have been a social misfit to begin with, so she continued reading to see what others had to say. 'I never would have met my perfect Dominant if it hadn't been for my training. He says I'm the best submissive he's ever had. Thanks a million!'

Finally, she found what she thought was more of a negative review. 'Taking this course helped me understand that submission is *not* my thing. At least I didn't waste years of my life trying to be something I'm not.'

Brie went back to the photo of the woman bound to the table. If she was totally honest with herself, what she really wanted was to be that woman…

Against her better judgment, Brie wrote an enquiring email to the Training Center. Before she could have any second thoughts, she hit the send button. As soon as she'd done so, she groaned loudly. *Great, now they have my email address!*

She tossed and turned all night, worried about the email she'd sent, even though part of her couldn't wait to get a reply. Brie let herself fantasize that she was on the table, with the man at the tobacco shop as her partner. She played with herself but couldn't get off. She was unable to get a restful sleep because of it and woke up cranky the next day.

Unfortunately, Brie had to wait until after her shift to check for a reply. She was thrilled when she found an email from the Center.

Dear Miss Bennett,

Thank you for your enquiry. Our campus is on the bottom floor of a larger school. The same institution runs both. As you probably read on the website, the Training Center has been running for over twenty-five years. Unlike most learning institutions, we guarantee complete satisfaction. If you are not happy with the training received, you are entitled to a full refund. We believe that strongly in what we do here.

The tuition is five thousand dollars for the six-week course. If you are unable to pay the amount, I suggest you apply for our scholarship program. I will include an application form in the packet. To apply for the program itself, you will need to provide your mailing address. There is an extensive questionnaire you must fill out, as well as a required homework assignment.

If you are accepted into the school, you can expect to start immediately. The classes take place every night from seven until midnight on weeknights and from three until midnight on Saturdays. The rigorous schedule allows us to pack as much as possible into the six-week span.

You asked what the benefits are of taking our exclusive training. Our program is the best of its kind. We like to think of ourselves as providers of Geisha training for submissives. Our students learn the art of submission, but they also learn their personal limits.

It is a safe environment where students are given the tools and experience to fulfill their submissive tendencies. Of note: our graduates are sought by respected Dominants around the world because of their extensive training. Truly, it is a unique opportunity.

Let me know if I can be of further service to you.

Sincerely,
Rachael Dunningham

Brie felt a prickling sensation after reading the email. It was the feeling she got whenever she stumbled onto something big. She spent the rest of the night googling information on submissives and Dominants. Some of what she read frightened her, but the majority of it made her want to investigate further.

Homework

B rie could appreciate how finding one's limits in six weeks might be beneficial, not only for the submissives but for the Dominants interested in them. She sent a reply and gave Rachael her mailing address. She figured it couldn't hurt to get additional information. She expected to get the packet in the mail within a week, but was pleased when it arrived the following day.

She poured the contents of the envelope onto her kitchen table. Rachael hadn't been kidding about there being a ton of paperwork to fill out. There was also a thin box included. Brie opened it up and slid out the contents. It turned out to be a red, eight-inch stick about the circumference of her index finger, with what looked like an upside-down heart attached to the end. It resembled a thin little penis, and it made her laugh.

Brie glanced through the pamphlets, which pretty much included the same information she'd found on the website. Then she found instructions for her 'homework'. It was downright shocking. The instructions stated that, as an applicant, Brie was required to send a video of herself using the little red phallus. She was expected to suck on it as if it were a cock, use it to excite her pussy, and then stimulate her anus with it. That last step sent a cold chill through Brie. As far as she was concerned, her ass was off limits. Having anything shoved up there was totally unnatural and potentially painful.

She gathered all the materials and threw them in the trash. Brie was unhappy that this 'school' now had her email *and* mailing address. How stupid could she be? If she had any problems whatsoever, she would call the Better Business Bureau *and* the cops.

For the rest of the week, she was on pins and needles, waiting to be contacted by the Training Center or visited by the man who had left the business card. Nothing happened. When the weekend rolled around, Brie called the BBB anyway and was relieved to learn there had been no complaints filed against the school.

She took the packet out of the trash and looked it over again. The questions intrigued her and she soon found herself filling it out—not to send in, but to get to know herself better.

One of the first questions was, 'What types of men do you like, and what qualities are most attractive?' Along the same vein, 'What types of men would you prefer not to have sex with, and what qualities turn you off?' The packet also asked about sexual experiences, such as, 'How old were you when you lost your virginity?', 'How many partners have you been with?' and 'Describe the best sexual encounter you have ever had.' There was even a section listing different sexual acts. For that section, there were five options to check: 'Like', 'Interested', 'Neutral', 'Don't Like' and 'Don't Know'.

There were several practices Brie checked with a 'Like', including light bondage and dildo stimulation. Some she was 'Interested' in and a few she 'Didn't Like', such as anal sex and caning—seriously, being whacked with a cane did not sound pleasant.

Looking over her answers made Brie even more curious about the things she was interested in trying. The idea of being tied down and teased by her partner was a total turn-on. Whenever she thought of the man in the tobacco shop taking her that way, she instantly got wet.

Brie shoved the completed form back in the envelope, along with the humorous phallus, and put them in her closet. She wasn't going to send the packet in, but she liked the ideas it inspired. If she'd actually had a boyfriend she would have asked him to try some of them with her, but Brie was alone. Despite the fact that she had a pleasant face, a tight little body and an adventurous personality, she was dateless every weekend. Truly, the world was a fucked-up place.

She had the late shift on Saturday. Although it was fairly busy during the afternoon, at around six o'clock, the place became an utter tomb. She watched the clock as time dragged by, minute by painful minute. *This is it—this is the extent of my sad little existence.* The only appealing aspect of her life was making her film shorts, which nobody watched.

Brie bent over the counter with her chin resting in her hands. *I want more.* The voice in her head was demanding and clear. Life was too precious to wish it away, hoping things would change.

Late that night, she fished the packet out of the closet and took the small phallus in her hand. She looked it over. It seemed harmless enough. She decided to record herself, knowing she could erase it if she didn't feel comfortable. Brie initially chose only to do the first two parts of the instructions. She set up her video camera in her bedroom, adjusting it to get the proper angle. She made sure the lighting was perfect and then got partially dressed for the show.

Brie felt a bit of clothing would preserve her dignity and look sexier to boot. She wore a green camisole and a short, black skirt with no panties, so she had the ability to access the needed area without exposing herself. She also chose an angle that would not display her pussy to the camera. Whoever watched it would be able to see her actions without seeing all of her. Brie was a professional—she wasn't about to make a porno.

She pressed the record button and lay down on the bed. She looked at the camera shyly and then turned away. She wasn't going to play for the camera. No, she wanted to pretend that it wasn't there, that this was just her, alone, playing by herself.

Brie couldn't help smiling when she brought the red stick to her lips. It was just so thin and long. *Talk about a pencil dick.* She laughed and then began licking the heart-shaped head of the phallus. Brie closed her eyes so she could imagine that it was a cock she was teasing with her mouth. She twirled her tongue around the head and nibbled up the sides of the shaft. She sucked on just the tip and then slowly, ever so slowly took the length of it, centimeter by centimeter, into her mouth. The eight-inch toy was too long for her so she didn't even attempt to take it all the way. Once it was comfortably in her mouth, she began thrusting it in and out as if it belonged to a real man. She made little mewing sounds, getting into the fantasy. Brie snuck a hand down between her legs and was surprised that she was actually wet.

She got on her hands and knees and held the phallus upright. She could just imagine the man at the tobacco shop lying on her bed with a raging hard-on, wanting her to suck him. She purred as her lips came down on the tiny cock, taking as much as she could without gagging. Brie moved up and down on it vigorously, stopping every now and then to tease the head with her teeth. She was getting horny and wanted desperately for the man to stuff his cock inside her.

Since that wasn't going to happen, Brie lay on her back and snaked the red toy down to her wet little mound. She lifted her hips up and teased the outside of her pussy with it.

She closed her eyes again and pretended her partner was teasing her with his massive dick. He brushed it against her clit, rubbing it several times to make her ready for deep penetration. Then he rubbed the head of his cock around her opening, tempting her by barely entering and then backing away. She drove herself wild with her teasing. Finally, she allowed herself to push the phallus inside. At first, it was a major disappointment. She was so wet and loose that she couldn't get any stimulation from it. She needed more girth to be satisfied.

Brie changed tactics and began exploring herself with the phallus. How far could it go in without being uncomfortable? It turned out that, in her excited state, all the way and then some... She rubbed different areas of her vagina with the head, using various angles to find what felt good. There was one spot in particular on the roof of her vagina that treasured the attention. She began thrusting the phallus inside, keeping that angle.

She continued to pretend that the man from the shop was fucking her hard with his large shaft. He was relentless, taking her for his own pleasure, but giving her pleasure in return. When she caught herself moaning, she instantly shut up. *How silly—moaning over a stick.*

Brie pulled the tiny phallus out and examined it. It was covered in her womanly juices and looked exceedingly thin. She cocked her head, considering whether it was small enough not to hurt going inside her virginal ass. For a brief second, her insides contracted in pleasure at the thought. *Maybe it won't be so bad.*

However, Brie wouldn't do it without lubricant. She jumped off the bed and turned off the camera, throwing sweats over her clothes. Fifteen minutes later, after a quick run to the store, she was back and recording, with a tube of gel in hand.

She lay back on the bed and then giggled when she noticed she'd left her socks on. Brie quickly peeled them off and threw them across the room, making a basket in the hamper. "Score!" she yelled. She looked back at the camera and grinned.

The tube of gel was a bit intimidating. She'd never used lube before, and associated it with nasty anal sex. Now Brie was about to introduce herself to nasty anal sex, and it scared her a little. At least she was in control and could stop if it hurt.

She coated the thin red shaft with an overabundance of gel. For good measure, she rubbed the excess over her tight little hole. Knowing she was being recorded, Brie tried to rub her asshole sensually. Before long, she was actually enjoying the sensation, and she pushed just the tip of her middle finger inside. She was surprised at how tight and warm it was, but her anus resisted her invasion.

By then, Brie was turned on enough to want more. The idea of introducing a foreign object into this forbidden part of her body made her juices flow. She took a deep breath and positioned the plastic phallus.

The head, which had been laughably small, now seemed much too large. It was almost the width of one and a half fingers. She pushed it against her tight sphincter and felt her body clam up accordingly. "Relax," she said out loud. She took several deep, calming breaths. Closing her eyes to concentrate, she imagined her tobacco man's cock pushing against her ass. He wanted access to her. He longed to take her in this most intimate way, and she *wanted* him to have her.

She got onto her hands and knees to better play out the scenario. Brie reached around and positioned the phallus again. In her mind, she rocked against his shaft, wanting him inside her, needing to hear his grunts and groans of pleasure. With a little more effort, the tip of the phallus slipped in. She gasped and stopped. It felt strange, and not necessarily sexy. She closed her eyes again, and her imaginary lover told her how tight she was. He was about to come just being inside her, but she wasn't ready. She pushed the shaft in deeper. She could feel every part of it. For the first time, she was grateful for the size of the tiny phallus. Anything bigger would have scared her away from trying.

How far can I take it? With no need to rush, Brie slowly inserted most of the thin shaft inside her. She arched her back and could feel the phallus press against new places. How would it feel to really be taken in the ass? She took hold of the end and started pulling it out. Her body tightened around the head as if it was reluctant for the toy to leave. That was certainly a new sensation for her. She pushed it back in and felt the same resistance. Either way, her body tightened.

Brie took it slowly, sliding the shaft in and out of herself. Still imagining her mystery man was taking her, she began moaning softly. He wanted to come inside her ass, covering the inside of her with his essence. "Yes…" she whispered. Faster now, she thrust it even deeper. The more she thrust, the more relaxed her body became. She laid her head down for support so that she could continue thrusting while she played with her clit. "Take me, Sir. Take me deeper," she murmured.

Brie rubbed her clit vigorously as she imagined him thrusting without mercy into her ass. The heat between her legs grew into an inferno. He was ready to come. He grabbed her buttocks and pushed in so deep that it made her scream. "Yes, Sir, oh, yes!" she panted. Her pussy began contracting in rhythmic waves as her orgasm consumed her. She stopped her hand movements as she enjoyed the ride. When it finally ended, she slowly pulled the phallus out.

Brie jumped off the bed and walked up to the camera. "I guess I'm finished with my homework." She chuckled softly as she turned it off.

She'd never had that much fun by herself before. What would it be like to actually have a partner? She shivered pleasantly at the thought.

Brie sat down and watched the entire thing, wondering if it needed editing. Just watching herself made her hot again. She decided not to make any cuts and burned it onto a DVD. She grabbed the paperwork and the financial form and slipped them in an envelope. She mailed it the next day by certified mail. Now she just needed to wait and see if she qualified for a scholarship.

Class Begins

B rie did not have to wait long to hear back. She received a large package in the mail three days later. She knew it was good news as soon as she recognized the Submissive Training Center crest on the parcel. Brie tore into the box and the first thing she saw was a letter:

Dear Miss Bennett,

We are happy to inform you that you've qualified for a full scholarship to the Submissive Training Center. Your entry was among the finest received by the school to date. We firmly believe the opportunity provided by our school will benefit you, now and in the future.

As stated when you first contacted us, you will begin the course immediately. Class starts tomorrow at 7:00 PM. You must be prompt and ready to learn. A school uniform has been provided.

Understand that this six-week course is a rigorous undertaking. We will expect much from you but promise expert training in return.

Sincerely,
Thane Davis

The letter had the most exquisite handwriting. Brie couldn't believe a man had penned it and wondered if Thane Davis was the gentleman she'd met at the tobacco shop.

She lifted the tissue paper away, expecting something similar to a high school uniform; instead, she found a miniskirt and leather top with laces up the front like a corset—both were dark brown. Also included was a pair of six-inch heels, some crotchless pantyhose with sexy seams up the back, and a red thong. The next item she pulled out was a tailored black trenchcoat. At the bottom of the box was an elaborate makeup kit with instructions to emphasize her eyes and lips. The instructions also noted that she was to wear her hair down.

Brie was ecstatic about trying the uniform on. She didn't really own sexy clothes. She was a filmmaker at heart, so a loose-fitting, not-too-flashy ensemble was the norm. As she slipped on the skirt and zipped it up, she finally understood why they had asked for body measurements in the paperwork. Each piece of clothing fit perfectly.

It took a bit of adjusting to get the seam of her hose to go up her leg in a straight line. She slipped into the heels and almost toppled over when she stood up. Dang, the heels were hell to walk in. She stood in front of the mirror and looked herself over. The skirt was almost scandalous and the top accentuated the round fullness of her breasts. Those difficult heels did a real number on her legs, making her calves look shapely and elegant. The seam of the hose created a sensual trail for the eyes to follow. Everything about the outfit made her feel like a woman—a hot, sexy woman!

She undid her ponytail and tossed her hair back and forth. Brie looked into the mirror again and saw an entirely different person looking back. This woman was alluring, more confident and ready to please. She wondered what would happen if she walked out of her apartment dressed like this. Brie giggled, realizing the necessity of the coat. She reluctantly took off her uniform and laid it over a chair to keep it wrinkle free for her first day of class.

Getting through another tedious day at work was the ultimate torture. Brie was both excited and nervous about the upcoming session. Not knowing what the school was like or what would be expected of her was daunting. She was also wondering about the other students. Would they be friendly and helpful, or back-stabbing bitches?

She asked to leave a half-hour early. Mr. Reynolds, being the sweetie that he was, let her go and took the last part of her shift. Brie wanted time to get her clothes on and her makeup just right. Even though she had printed directions to the school, she left early to leave extra time in case she got lost. Being prompt was important to her.

It took twenty minutes to arrive at the campus. The Training Center looked like any other community college. The parking lot was full of cars and normal-looking college students milling just outside the large brick building. Nothing about the older building hinted as to what was happening inside. Brie got out of her car and tightened the belt of her coat around her waist. She stumbled a couple of times as she made her way to the entrance. *God, I hate high heels!*

A young man opened the door as she approached. *Now, that is a pleasant change.* She smiled at him and nodded in appreciation. Inside, she saw an information desk and headed directly to it. The woman at the desk smiled and asked, "Can I help you?"

"Where do I go for the…Training Center?" Brie was embarrassed to say the full name in public.

"It's one floor down. Just take the elevator to your right."

"Thanks." She was about to leave, but turned around and asked, "What kind of school is on this floor?"

The receptionist smiled brightly. "It's a business college. Are you interested in applying to it as well?"

Brie shook her head. "No, just curious. Thanks for your help."

"Anytime. Enjoy your first day."

Brie sighed nervously. This was it—there was no turning back. She hit the button in the elevator and watched the doors slowly close. She was curious about what the Training Center would look like. Would it be one giant room with many beds and tools of the trade hanging on the walls, or would it have small, individual rooms with beds and curtains for privacy? Brie held her breath as the doors opened, and then laughed out loud. The elevator opened to a large commons area. It was lined by normal-looking classrooms with desks and large whiteboards. Brie shook her head. Definitely *not* what she had been expecting.

She stepped out of the elevator and looked around. A tall woman in a harsh business suit came up to her and demanded, "What class are you taking?"

Brie got out her schedule and looked for her first class so she could answer. "It's called Submission 101."

The woman pointed. "Go down that hall. It's the last door on the left. Hurry, you don't want to be late."

Brie quickly made her way down the hall, which was a mistake on her part. Her ankle rolled and she found herself on the floor. She picked herself up and continued on, not daring to look back at the woman. *Damn, I hate these shoes!*

She walked into the classroom and saw that there were five other women already seated. The instructor, a tiny man wearing a nametag that said 'Mr. Gallant', indicated where she should sit. She made her way to the desk and sat down, breathing a sigh of relief. At least she'd made it to class on time.

"Miss Bennett, since you are the last to arrive I see no reason to wait until the bell rings. Let's begin. We have a lot to get through tonight." Her instructor had silver highlights in his hair and a wiry frame. Although the man was small, he had a commanding voice and demeanor. The two-hour class was devoted to defining and classifying who and what submissives were.

In a short period of time, Brie learned the difference between submissives and slaves. "Understand that a submissive *volunteers* and is allowed to voice preferences and set personal limits. Slaves give up those rights." Brie knew right then that she would never be a slave. The whole idea set her on edge.

"There are various levels of submission, but we will only talk about the major three. Light submissives give of themselves for short durations, setting many boundaries around what they will and won't do. Even though they submit to their Dominants, they still maintain a high level of control. Moderate submissives put fewer limitations on their Dominants and are interested in living the D/s lifestyle for longer periods of time. They offer the Doms a more significant level of control. You should note that most submissives fall under this category. Then there are those few who are heavily submissive. Such submissives desire one full-time Master and set *very* few limitations on the Dominant. It is similar to acting as a slave, but the submissive still has control—he or she just chooses not to use it."

Brie wrote down everything he said. Although she'd read similar information on the web, he defined things in a way that was easier to understand.

"Miss Bennett, have you ever heard of the term 'sub-space'?" Mr. Gallant asked.

Brie looked around, wishing he had called on someone else. "Sorry, no."

"That's fine," the tiny man answered. "This is an introduction course. In fact, if we go over any information you have questions about, be sure to stop and ask. You cannot offend me with what you do not know."

Brie nodded in gratitude. She really liked him as an instructor. Mr. Gallant's voice commanded her attention and he seemed to care about his students. A silly thought flitted through her head: *What if he is a Dominant in real life?* She wondered what it would be like to have him as a partner. Brie actually blushed and had to refocus on his lesson.

"The term 'subspace' refers to a trancelike state experienced by many submissives. Certain types of 'play' can help pump endorphins into the bloodstream, making the submissive open to more intensive stimulation. While in that state, the sub must rely on the Dominant's vigilance because of the higher pain tolerance. In fact, the sub may become incapable of verbal communication while floating in subspace, making him or her completely dependent on the Dominant during and immediately following such intense play. Naturally, a high level of trust is required between partners."

To Brie, subspace sounded like a frightening experience. To lose control like that and be at the mercy of another person's whims seemed unacceptable. It made her wonder if she wasn't submissive material after all.

"Ladies, it is imperative you understand that a *true* submissive finds pleasure in serving the needs and desires of another. If it is more about your needs than your Dom's, then it is just roleplaying in the bedroom."

After that profound statement, Mr. Gallant ended the class. "It is time for your first practicum. Please leave your coat at your desk and proceed to room eight, at the other end of the hall."

Brie looked at the other five women nervously and then undid her coat. She slipped it off her shoulders and laid it across her desk. The other women followed suit. Each had on a different outfit. Some were made of leather of different colors, similar to hers, while others were made of satin and lace. Brie wondered if any thought had been given to each individual uniform, or if they had all been randomly selected. Whatever the case, all of the women looked scandalously stunning in their uniforms.

The five filed out and she followed behind them. Just as she made it to the door, Brie stumbled and slammed against the doorframe.

"Miss Bennett, I recommend that you get used to walking in those shoes. Tomorrow I want you to wear them as soon as you get up and practice walking in them the entire day. Consider it your homework assignment."

Brie wanted to protest, to explain why that wasn't practical given her place of employment. However, the kindness in his eyes made her stop and reconsider. Mr. Gallant wanted her to succeed with her training and, for whatever reason, six-inch heels were important to him. She nodded and smiled before attempting to walk down the hall with grace.

It turned out that room eight was *not* a normal class-room. There was a table at the front with four instructors already seated at it. The floor was made of a soft, spongy material and, in the middle of the room, Brie noticed six odd pillows that looked like large triangles lying on their sides. She had no idea what they were used for, but they certainly weren't for sitting on.

"Take your place behind of one of the ramps."

Brie looked up at the sound of a familiar voice. Her heart started racing upon seeing the object of her fantasies sitting in front of her.

"Tonight we shall weed out the wannabe sub-misssives."

There was a collective gasp in the room. Brie looked at each of the four instructors, wondering what that meant. The panel consisted of three men and one woman. The woman was the same one who had met her off the elevator. She looked serious and severe, although she was striking, with long, blonde hair. The two other men were polar opposites. The man on the end was tanned and large—in a bodybuilder sort of way—while the one next to him was a skinny man with dark eyes and pale skin. Unfortunately, none of their faces gave a hint as to what 'weeding out' meant.

A fellow student spoke up. "What are you saying exactly?"

"You may address me as Sir. That goes for all of you," he replied, looking directly at Brie. She trembled under his gaze.

There was silence in the room until the girl said, "Yes, Sir."

He nodded and answered her question. "Similar to in Ivy League institutions, your first few classes are designed to discourage the weak. We are only interested in training true submissives. You may choose to leave the program at any time, or you may be asked to leave by any one of your instructors."

"What about our tuition?" the girl complained.

"It will be returned in full. Let me reiterate, we are only interested in true submissives. Some of you are unable to identify if you are true submissives yet. Tonight we hope to make that abundantly clear." He held up their application packets. "We have your personal lists of preferences and dislikes," he stated. "The men chosen for this first practicum were picked based on your responses."

Brie couldn't breathe. They were going to have sex in front of the instructors, right now? She looked down at the pillow in front of her and suddenly realized what it was. If she were to lie face down on it, the edge of the ramp would lift her ass into the air at the perfect height for fucking.

An assistant came into the room and handed each of the girls a black strip of cloth.

"Tie on the blindfold and lie down on the ramp."

Sir's authoritative tone spurred her to comply. She looked over at the other women. All of them looked as shocked as she was. Brie covered her eyes and tied the blindfold tightly around her head. Then she knelt down and felt for the ramp.

It was firmer than she'd expected, but the spongy floor made kneeling comfortable. She pressed her waist against the edge of the 'ramp' and laid her torso down on the large pillow. The angle of it made her head lower than her pelvis. She could just imagine her ass in the air, as if she were begging to be fucked. Brie sighed nervously, silently hoping Sir would be the one to take her.

She heard the men enter the room and felt the tension rise. None of the men spoke, but she sensed that one was standing behind her. A tingling sensation coursed through her body as she realized a complete stranger was about to have sex with her.

Brie felt his hands reach under her skirt and peel off her little thong. She bit her lip, keeping silent. She heard him unzip his pants and remove them slowly. Brie started hyperventilating when the man knelt down next to her and grabbed her ass cheeks. He positioned his cock against her opening and waited.

She could hear the other men moving, and some of the girls gasped. Then there was silence. Sir's voice was low and sensual. "Miss Bennett, you indicated that you were turned off by men over the age of fifty."

She automatically stiffened. "Yes, Sir."

"Meet your partner."

The man with his cock pressed against her spoke. "My name is Greg, and I am sixty-eight."

Brie heard the girl who had asked about tuition suddenly shout, "Is mine fat?"

"Yes, Miss Evans, he is." Brie heard scuffling and then the dull thud of heels on the matting as the girl ran from the room. Brie was distracted by it until Greg began pushing his shaft into her. All her attention immediately focused on him as the man slowly penetrated her with the head of his cock.

He took his time with Brie, letting her adjust to his length, giving her time to enjoy the feel of his manhood moving inside her. Once his cock was fully engulfed by her moist walls, he began thrusting. Greg held down her hips in a way that allowed his cock deeper access. She found that it didn't matter that he was old enough to be her grandfather—her body responded to him eagerly. She bit her lip again, resisting the urge to cry out in pleasure and embarrass herself.

"That's it, lass. Milk my cock with that hot little pussy."

Brie moaned softly, so softly that she doubted anyone but her partner could hear it. She heard the grunts and cries of the other couples in the room. There was something so primal about copulating in the presence of other people. She forgot about the panel watching her as she pushed against his shaft, taking him even deeper. Brie wanted to be possessed by his manhood, to be used for his pleasure.

He slapped her ass, making her yelp. "Good. I want to hear you, pet."

Greg took hold of her waist and started pounding with vigor. Brie cried out at the intensity of his thrusts, but again she bit her lip to silence herself. If she truly let go, she would sound like a wild animal.

By the sounds of the grunting going on in the room, some of the men were already finishing off. She felt her pussy contract in pleasure in response to their noises.

Brie found it sexually exciting to give herself to this stranger. She realized his age didn't matter. It was the way he handled her, the way he derived his pleasure from her that had her so wet and horny. "Oooh…" she moaned.

Her moan must have triggered his orgasm, because he stiffened for a second and then started pounding her without restraint. The room filled with the sounds of their flesh slapping against each other as he possessed her with his cock. She took all of him, reveling in the feel of his climax. When he finally pulled out, she sighed inwardly, wanting more of him.

"Take off your blindfolds and thank your partners," Sir instructed.

Brie slipped the cloth down around her neck and turned her head. Greg looked every bit his age, with his wrinkly skin, gray hair and a hollow face, but it didn't matter. She'd enjoyed their encounter. "Thank you, Greg."

He fingered a strand of her curly brown hair. "My pleasure, pet."

The men dressed themselves and left while Sir talked to the students. "That was a good start, class. As you noticed, we have already lost one of you. I expect there will be a few more casualties tonight." He looked at each of the girls individually, as if they were the next in line to go. Brie shivered under his gaze.

"Dress and stand before the panel," he ordered. Brie lifted herself off the ramp and put her little red thong back on. It was slightly moist and smelled of her. She thought back on her little tryst and smiled.

When all five girls were standing in a line, Sir began the critiques. "Ms. Clark, any comments on Miss Bennett's performance?"

Brie was surprised when the severe instructor looked at her and smiled. "Overall, I was pleased. It is obvious that she enjoyed the experience, which in turn pleased her partner."

The burly man on the end spoke up. "I was concerned that she was so silent. Her partner indicated that he wanted her to make more vocalizations, but she didn't."

Sir jumped on his comment. "I agree, Master Coen. I noticed she bit her lip on several occasions. Explain yourself, Miss Bennett."

Brie was shaking, embarrassed at being criticized in front of everyone. "I didn't want to sound like an idiot, Sir. I was trying to be sensual."

"Nonsense. Your partner encouraged you to be vocal and you denied him that. Don't let it happen again. Unless your Dom specifically tells you to be silent, you need to let him hear your pleasure and pain. How can he adjust to your needs unless you do that?"

Brie wanted to disappear, but she whispered, "Sorry, Sir."

The ghostlike instructor spoke up. "Although I agree that her lack of vocalizations was a problem, it was obvious to me that his age did not affect her ability to please or to be pleased by him. Bravo, Miss Bennett." She smiled at him, grateful for his praise. However, his dark gaze caused her loins to contract in fearful pleasure. She was surprised he had that kind of power over her and looked down at her feet.

Each of the remaining girls received critiques of a similar nature. All had weaknesses that the panel highlighted and addressed. It was a humbling experience, to say the least.

When they had finished, Sir spoke to the class as a whole. "We will discuss your performance amongst ourselves. Make your way to the commons area. There you will find refreshments. Wait until I come for you."

Brie stumbled twice before she made it out of the room. She heard Sir call out to her, "Shoes!" She turned to him and nodded, humiliated at being called out like that. She gritted her teeth and tried to walk away with grace. *Damn these fucking shoes!*

The Second Practicum

The commons was in the center of the building. It had been set up with wine, beer, finger foods and miniature desserts. *A girl's dream.* All five of the women were silent as they gathered what they wanted and sat at a nearby table. Once they were seated, Brie spoke up. "Well, that was different." There was nervous laughter all around. The group quietly consumed their refreshments, each mulling over what had just happened.

It didn't seem real that Brie had been taken by a stranger—and not just any stranger. The man had been the exact opposite of what she found attractive. It had been a shocking test, but it had opened her eyes. Age did not hold the importance she'd thought it did. What else would she find out about herself?

Sir came to the commons area a short time later. "I want to speak to you each individually before we begin the next practicum. Miss Sanders," he said, directing a small brunette to join him at a far-off table.

The conversation between them looked intense, and the prospect of speaking to Sir alone like that made Brie nervous. She took another sip of wine to build her courage.

All the other women were called up to talk to him before she finally got her chance. She subconsciously bit her lip as she tried to walk gracefully in her heels. There was only a slight wobble near the end and she prayed he hadn't noticed.

"I saw your video," he stated when she sat down. Brie blanched a little. What was he going to say about it? "I am curious. It says on your application that you do not like anal sex." She nodded slowly in agreement. "Why, then, did you use the dildo in such a manner?"

"The instructions said to."

A smile tugged at the corner of his lips. "No, they did not. You were only instructed to stimulate your anus."

Brie's eyes widened. "You mean I didn't have to?"

"No. But the fact that you did says a lot about you."

She closed her eyes, feeling sick. *What does it say about me?* Did he think she was a slut, or maybe a liar?

"Look at me." Brie opened her eyes and saw Sir staring at her kindly. "You believed you did not like anal sex, although you hadn't tried it. It was obvious in your video." Brie wondered what he meant by that, but was afraid to ask. "I think there is a lot you don't know about yourself, Miss Bennett."

Brie's bottom lip quivered. "I think you are right, Sir."

"We plan to strip away any misconceptions you have in the next few weeks. You may find out things about yourself that will shock you. Are you prepared for that?"

"I don't know, Sir."

His chuckle was low and lighthearted. It delighted her to hear it. "Fair enough. I see great potential in you, but you will need to trust our guidance and be true to your instincts. Don't try to be or do something that doesn't come naturally. Be authentic and you will help the process go much faster. Do you understand?"

"Yes, Sir. I'm actually looking forward to it."

"Fine." He stood up, and she followed suit. Sir casually rested his hand on the small of her back as he addressed the group. Brie struggled to hear his words because all she could concentrate on was his touch. Her whole body vibrated, as if an electrical current was grounding her.

"Follow me to the auditorium. We have something special planned for each of you."

Sir removed his hand and walked ahead of the group. It was as if the electricity had suddenly been turned off, and Brie struggled to move. All she wanted was for Sir to touch her again.

A lanky blonde in black leather moved in close to her and growled under her breath, "Bitch!"

And it starts… Brie wasn't surprised that the other girls had noticed his gesture, nor was she shocked that some of them resented it. She stumbled as her ankle rolled again. The blonde laughed at her expense, gliding across the floor flawlessly in her six-inch heels. *Stupid cow.*

The auditorium was circular, with a small stage in the center and rows of seats all around it. The other instructors were already there, waiting for them. The small group was directed to sit in the front row.

"Once again, your partner has been chosen based on the questionnaire you filled out. This time, however, we will *all* watch your performance." He nodded towards the students. "We want you to observe and learn from each other."

Brie was excited at the prospect of watching the other girls. She just hoped she wasn't the first one called up.

Luckily, Sir called Miss Sanders' name and told her to go up onto the stage. The small brunette walked up the steps timidly. Brie could tell she was shaking like a leaf and clapped her hands in support. Several of the other girls joined her—except Blonde Nemesis, of course.

Sir spoke in a smooth, calming tone. "Miss Sanders, you stated that you dislike the idea of being whipped."

"Yes, Sir," she answered in a barely audible whisper.

"You also mentioned you like your men clean-shaven and hairless."

This time Sanders only nodded. Brie knew where this was headed and was not surprised to see a large, muscular man walk onto the stage in only his briefs. He had a beard, and fur covered his chest and arms. Not only that, but he held a crop in his hand—the kind used for whipping horses during a race.

Brie heard the clanking of chains as they were lowered from the ceiling above the stage. All of the girls looked up in awe and fear, including Sanders.

The Dom put the whip in her mouth and commanded her to hold it. He then took Sanders' left wrist and buckled it into a leather cuff attached to the chain above her head. He took her other wrist and did the same. The large man undid the ties of her corset and let it fall to the floor, peeling off her panties last before retrieving the whip from her mouth. Sanders stood before their little group, naked and bound.

Brie held her breath as the Dom circled his sub, snapping the crop against his hand repeatedly. She watched Sanders, wondering if the girl would call it off and quit. Brie was surprised to see an expression of lustful fear on her face.

The man started running the leather tongue of the crop against Sanders' skin. Brie heard her whimper, but the tone of it was ripe with excitement. Everyone in the room knew she wanted what was coming. Her Dom snapped the whip against her right ass cheek and she cried out in satisfaction. He quickly followed it up with a snap on her left butt cheek. The crack of the whip echoed in the small auditorium.

He moved to her front and ran the crop over her small breasts. Brie couldn't believe he was going to do it, but then he did. The Dom snapped it down on her nipple. Sanders cried out in painful pleasure, and he grunted. "You like that, don't you?" She nodded her head meekly.

"Tell me what you want."

"I want you to whip me again...please."

Before her last word was out, he cracked it over her other nipple. Sanders' whimpering cry was erotic, and Brie felt a wave of wetness between her legs. She was stunned that she found the whipping scene so arousing.

She snuck a glance at Sir and saw that he was watching Sanders intently. He scribbled something down in his notebook while the Dom continued to whip and tease

Sanders to distraction. Brie turned her eyes back to the stage and watched as he bent over, cupping Sanders' chin to kiss her on the lips. The chains made clinking noises as she attempted to move away from his kiss.

Sir asked, "Is she wet?"

The Dom reached his hand between her legs and growled. "Oh, yes, she's dripping."

"You may release her."

He took Sanders out of the bindings with tenderness. The way he treated her afterwards was gentle, as if he were her lover. Sanders swayed a little as she found her legs again. It was clear she was weak from the erotic tryst. Her Dom stood next to her protectively.

Sir stood up and addressed her. "Miss Sanders, how do you feel right now?"

"Excited, a little off balance."

"Would you want the Dom to continue with the whipping?"

"Yes," she answered without hesitation.

"Good. Thank him and sit back down."

Sanders opened her mouth to thank him, but the Dom said clearly, "Suck me."

She looked back over at Sir questioningly, but his expression was unreadable. Sanders obediently sank to her knees and eased his large cock out of his briefs. She wrapped her small hand around his shaft and opened her mouth wide. Her slurping sounds filled the room as she sucked on his manhood. He put his hand on the back of her head, forcing her to take it even deeper. "That's good. Swallow my come, little dove."

When Sanders had swallowed the last of his essence,

she stood up. They exchanged a look that surprised Brie. The Dom clearly had affection for Sanders and she had seemed to enjoy the way he played with her, but she was obviously turned off by his looks.

Sir spoke to her again. "Miss Sanders, would you have preferred this scene had played out with somebody else?"

She answered quickly, "Yes."

The hairy man nodded to Sir and walked off the stage. The chains disappeared upwards, clinking ominously. Sanders quickly donned her clothes and returned to her seat. The four remaining girls waited for their names to be called.

"Miss Bennett."

Brie felt a chill go through her. What did Sir have in store for her this time around?

Brie's Breakthrough

S he climbed the stairs onto the stage and faced the panel bravely.

"Class," Sir said, looking at the other women. "Miss Bennett shared in her application that she was bullied by classmates at the predominantly African American school she attended as a child. Because of that, she has an unnatural fear of anyone of African American descent." Sir looked up at Brie. "Is this true, Miss Bennett?"

Brie nodded, cursing herself for putting it in the application. As if Sir could read her mind, he said, "Do not regret telling us your background. The more we know about you, the faster your training will advance. Hiding parts of yourself will only lead to difficulties later on. Do you understand?"

"Yes, Sir."

"You noted that you do not like anal sex. Why?"

She looked down at her feet. "I've never tried it, Sir. Truthfully, I don't know if I like it or not, but it sounds painful."

Sir looked at the group of women again. "Part of a Dominant's responsibility is to stretch and grow his sub without taking her too far."

Brie heard the steps of her new partner walking up the stairs. The man moved up behind her and wrapped his right arm around the front of her waist in a possessive manner. She looked down and was not surprised to see his skin was the color of dark chocolate.

His voice was a low rumble next to her ear. "Are you ready for me?"

Brie's breath came in short gasps. She wasn't prepared to do this... He turned her around and tilted her head up. "Are you ready?"

She looked up into his dark hazel eyes. Brie expected to see anger and hatred reflected in them, her irrational fear kicking in, but they were filled with lust—lust for her. She nodded. He grazed his thumb across her lips before his mouth came down on hers. His thick lips felt different and he had a spicier smell to his musk. Neither was unpleasant.

After the kiss, Brie's new Dom held her arm up and stroked the outline of her curves, causing her skin to tingle as his hand made its way down to her hip. His dark skin contrasted beautifully against her creamy white.

Having this man touch her intimately felt forbidden, even though her rational mind knew differently. She decided to give in to the feeling—wanting to feel wicked. When he kissed her again, she moaned into his mouth, letting his tongue claim her.

She heard movement on the stage. When he broke the embrace, she saw that a bed and small table had been placed near them. There were things laid out on the table, but she couldn't tell what.

The Dom began untying her leather top. Soon her chest was exposed to the audience. Brie looked away, not wanting to acknowledge that she had observers. She realized, however, that Sir was studying her with interest. She remembered his critique and made a conscious choice to be more vocal with this Dom.

She put her hand on the man's shoulder as he helped her step out of the skirt and hose. Then he lifted her up and placed her on the bed. "On all fours," he commanded. Brie saw the lubricant on the small table and began shaking all over. She struggled to breathe as she got on her hands and knees, frightened that what came next would hurt. A small whimper escaped her lips as he joined her on the bed.

Her Dom ran his hand over her back for reassurance. "There is no reason to be frightened. I'm not going to hurt you." He picked up an object from the table. "Have you seen one of these before?"

She looked at the item in his hand. It looked like a short phallus with a flanged end that was decorated with a large blue crystal. Brie answered quietly, "No."

He seemed amused and nodded his head. "It has an unromantic name, but is an enjoyable piece of equipment."

Brie tried to calm her erratic heartbeat. She was grateful that he was being understanding and patient with her. "What is it?" she asked.

"It's called a butt plug."

Brie looked up at him nervously.

Sir interrupted the scene to talk to the other students. "As you can see, her Dom has chosen a smaller device, since this is her first time." The other girls nodded as if they understood, but Brie couldn't miss the relief on their faces at knowing they weren't the ones up on stage.

She watched in a combination of fear and fascination as the Dom covered it in lubricant. "Lay your head on the pillow but keep your ass in the air. I want you to look back towards me."

Brie did as he asked, the position making her anus more accessible to him and easier for everyone else to see. She held her breath as he moved down between her legs. What he held in his hand was *way* bigger than the thing she had played with. She closed her eyes, determined to be brave.

"No, open them," he demanded gently.

She looked at him, realizing that being silent and shutting her eyes to get through it was not allowed. Her Dom needed and wanted Brie to communicate with him.

She fought the urge to bite her lip as she felt the cold tip of the plug push against her sphincter. She gasped when he slowly eased it inside her, stretching her tight hole, and then grunted in discomfort as he gently forced it farther in.

He pulled the plug out slightly and then pushed it back in. The movement seemed to loosen her muscles and the toy advanced farther inside her. He continued the process, moving slowly and allowing her body to adjust. Despite the small diameter of the plug, it felt as if there were a full-sized shaft inside her. She couldn't imagine what a real cock would feel like.

Brie panted as she continued to adjust to the ever-widening girth of the plug. Just when she didn't think her ass could stretch any more, she hit the stopper. Her anus clamped around it. The plug wasn't going anywhere until her Dom pulled it out. He bent down and kissed her ass cheeks. "It looks beautiful from here."

She envisioned her butt in the air, with a blue crystal where her asshole should be. Maybe it did look pretty. At least he was pleased. Brie tingled with a feeling of accomplishment. She'd taken the foreign object inside her. It certainly felt strange, but it did not hurt.

"Lie down on your back now," he growled lustfully.

She shivered with excitement, knowing he had something else in mind. She lay down and looked up at her handsome Dom. He looked so strong and powerful standing over her. She trembled when he pulled down his briefs and she saw his manhood for the first time. It was a lighter shade than the rest of him and incredibly thick. "I am going to take you with the plug still in place." He must have read the fear in her eyes, because he caressed her cheek and said, "Do you want to please me?"

Brie's loins quivered in response. Yes, she did want to please him, but not if it would hurt. She thought back to what Sir had said. He'd told the class that a good Dominant knew the limits of his or her sub. Did she trust this man not to harm her? She looked up into those hazel eyes again and had no doubt. She opened her legs to him.

Her dark-skinned Dom climbed between them. Even though she didn't mean to, she bit her lip when his cock entered her. His thickness would have filled her up on its own, but the added plug made her pussy so tight that it felt as if it were her first time.

He gently thrust his substantial girth inside her taut opening, allowing Brie's body to get used to the constricted feeling. After he'd fully penetrated her with his length, he began stroking her with his shaft. He used it like an instrument, rubbing her in places she hadn't been touched before. She vocalized for him then, letting him know how good it felt.

His thrusts became more focused and intense, rubbing on one spot in particular that gave her goose bumps. "Come for me. I want to feel your pussy come all over my dark shaft."

Brie moaned, wanting to give him her pleasure. She tilted her head back and started groaning deep in her throat. This was going to be an orgasm like none she had experienced before. Her whole body tensed right before the first intense wave hit. She screamed and then screamed again as the strength of it blurred her senses. For a moment, she lost track of everything—where she was, what she was doing, even who she was…

When Brie finally came back to earth, she became aware that he was still thrusting inside her. He leaned down and kissed her on the lips. "Good girl."

He grabbed onto her pelvis and pushed in as deep as her body could take him. She felt his cock pulse as he came inside her. It was so erotic that she cried out with him, wanting to share in his ecstasy.

The two lay there for several moments, catching their breath after such an intense session. Finally, he pulled away from her and then reached between her legs to slowly remove the plug. She felt empty when it was gone.

Brie rolled off the bed and stood up groggily, weak from their encounter.

"How do you feel right now?" Sir asked.

"Completely satisfied, Sir."

"Are you still afraid to take a man anally?"

She glanced at him, debating whether to be totally honest. "Yes, but not as much, Sir."

He gave a snorting laugh. "I appreciate your honesty, Miss Bennett. You appear to be taking our critiques to heart, although I was concerned when your Dom started to penetrate you and you clammed up."

Her Dom laughed, nodding in agreement. "Yes, she was a difficult read there for a bit, but I figured her out." He picked up the corset and started fastening it around Brie. Once she had her skirt zipped up, she gathered her hose, shoes, and panties to put on at her seat. She was about to skip off the stage when Sir reminded her curtly, "Thank your Dom."

Brie couldn't believe she'd forgotten. She put her items down and walked back to him with a smile on her lips. She was grateful that he had helped her to overcome one of her fears. "Thank you, um…Dom?"

He stroked her cheek with his thumb. "You may call me Baron."

"Thank you, Baron."

He kissed her one more time and then walked off the stage. She gathered her things and scooted down the stairs to take refuge in her seat.

Brie was shaken by the experience. So many new

things had happened in a short amount of time—it was too much to take in. She was barely aware when the next girl took the stage, or of the fact the girl ran out of the auditorium after quitting the program.

"Miss Bennett."

Brie ripped herself away from her inner thoughts. "Sir?"

"You are expected to observe each student so that you learn from them."

"I apologize, Sir."

"Are you okay, Miss Bennett?"

She sat up in her chair and tried to convey a sense of calm, although she was anything but. "I'm fine, Sir."

He whispered something to Ms. Clark, and then turned to Brie. "Let's talk outside." To the other girls he said, "Ms. Clark will call up the next student."

Brie quickly got to her feet and followed behind Sir. She heard the name 'Ms. Taylor' called and glanced back to see a girl with fake boobs and a pink corset get up on the stage.

Sir was silent until they were inside his office. He shut the door behind her before asking, "What are your thoughts?"

"I am having a paradigm shift, Sir. Everything that I thought I knew about myself seems to be wrong. Is this real, or am I deceiving myself because of the new environment?"

"I told you to follow your instincts. Have you been doing that?"

She shrugged. "Yes, but what does that prove?"

"Who you truly are is made clear when you respond

instinctively."

"But why wouldn't I know myself better by the age of twenty-two?"

He graced her with a charming grin. "You haven't been with the right people or in the right situations."

Brie looked down at the floor. "I feel so confused right now."

"Did you enjoy tonight?"

"Yes."

"Brie." It was the first time he'd called her by her first name. "I believe you are a rare commodity. You long to please the man you are with, no matter who he is. Now I want to test the limits of what you will do for him."

Having Sir speak to her so positively made her uncomfortable. For some reason, it was easier to be criticized than to be praised by him. "I would hate to disappoint you, Sir."

"Be yourself and you won't."

Brie nodded, relieved nothing more was required of her.

He asked, "Are you ready to finish your first day of training?"

She looked up at the clock and saw that there were less than thirty minutes left. "Yes, Sir."

They made their way back to the auditorium. Before they entered, Sir leaned towards her and said in an intimate whisper, "I will be the one to take your virginal bottom tomorrow."

Brie stopped in her tracks. The rush she felt was disconcerting. She forced herself to continue following him, but she stumbled in her shoes. He did not reprimand her, but she silently screamed at her shoes, *I will fucking conquer you!*

She stared at Sir exclusively as he recapped the evening's events and asked the panel of instructors to share their final thoughts. When midnight rolled around, Sir spoke to their dwindling class.

"Congratulations, submissives. You have survived your first day of training. We started with six and are now down to four. Look around you. I predict that after tomorrow, at least one of you will be gone. Get some rest—I promise tomorrow will be even more thrilling than today." Sir looked at Brie briefly, with a hint of a smile on his face, before he walked out of the room.

His smile did Brie in. She was consumed with the thought of being possessed by Sir. Tomorrow couldn't come soon enough.

Making an Impression

B rie woke up and immediately put on her six-inch heels as per the instructions of her teacher, Mr. Gallant. On her first day at the Submissive Training Center, she'd made a bad first impression by stumbling around. She was taking her homework assignment seriously, determined not to let those damn shoes embarrass her again.

While teetering on the impossible heels, she made a pot of coffee and ate a simple breakfast of toast with a sunny side up egg on top. Unfortunately, she rolled her ankle when transferring the egg from the stove onto her plate and felt a shooting pain travel up her leg. She ignored it—the shoes would not get the better of her. Her goal was to impress Sir.

He'd promised that tonight would be their first time together as Dom and submissive. The butterflies she felt just thinking about it made food difficult to swallow. After taking only a few bites, she threw her breakfast in the trash and got dressed for work.

When she entered the tobacco shop, Mr. Reynolds

coughed loudly and said, "Um, Brie, what's going on?"

"What?"

"You're overdressed for this place."

She looked down at the simple white blouse and purple skirt. Neither was remarkable, so she figured the shoes made the outfit seem sexier than it was. "Just felt like being a little different today."

He was staring at her legs in a way he never had before. It gave her a thrill, even it if was only Mr. Reynolds. "You might cause a few heart attacks among our older clientele," he commented before walking off.

Brie stifled a grin. A pair of shoes could make that kind of difference? *I never knew…*

She moved about the tiny shop more than usual, practicing her grace while walking. She had to slow her movements and as a result, everything she did felt more sensual. She even caught Jeff checking her out on several occasions. The lazy little shit suddenly became helpful, handing her merchandise with which to stock the shelves. It was amusing, but the boy was uncouth enough to stare at her ass without shame. She had to shoo him away.

Unfortunately, all of her practice left her feet excruciatingly sore by the end of her shift. Every step was so painful that she worried about stumbling just as badly as the first night.

The submissive training started at seven PM and lasted until midnight. She was required to wear a school uniform which included—of course—the damn shoes.

Brie applied her makeup with care and added a few extra curls to frame her young face. She wanted to look irresistible for Sir. They were going to couple that night in the most intimate of ways. He had promised to take her anal virginity and although the prospect was intimidating, the thought of having Sir as her partner made her wet with anticipation.

Not wanting to be late, she arrived at the Training Center fifteen minutes early. It took longer to walk to her class because of her aching feet. To her credit, she still moved with grace and made it to Mr. Gallant's class before the bell rang.

Sadly, there were only four girls now. Two had quit during the first day of training because the lessons had proved too challenging. She knew the first few days of training were designed to weed out any casual submissives, and wondered what this session would bring.

Brie looked around the room at the remaining women—Sanders (the small brunette with a secret whipping fetish), Blonde Nemesis (Brie's rival), and Ms. Taylor (the girl with the perky fake boobs). Based on what Sir had said the night before, at least one of them would leave the program by the end of the night. She wondered which of the three it would be, because there was *no way* it was going to be her.

Mr. Gallant started class five minutes before the bell rang. "As with last night, we have a lot to cover, so let us begin." The wiry little man walked around the room, observing the students carefully as he spoke. "You may think that being a submissive is purely a sexual act, but you would be wrong. Whenever a sub is in her Dom's presence, every movement, every word, even her eyes should convey her respect for the Dom. It doesn't matter where she is or what she is doing."

Brie raised her hand. When he eventually called on her, she asked, "But what if you are in public? Are you still supposed to bow and call him Master?"

"That would be foolish, unless your Dom has specifically asked you to behave in that manner. Normally, there is a different protocol depending on the environment. It is something you should discuss with your individual Doms."

Brie thought back to the beautiful redhead who had been with Sir at the tobacco shop. The only thing that had seemed odd between them was that she'd called him Sir. Otherwise, the two had seemed like an ordinary couple.

Mr. Gallant continued, "Tonight you will be learning basic commands and rules of etiquette. Although we will teach you what is commonly expected, your Dom's particular preference is the only thing that matters to you."

Blond Nemesis blurted her question without waiting to be called on. "So basically, we just do what we've been trained to do unless our Dom says differently?"

Mr. Gallant paused before answering, "Don't assume anything. Why take the risk of displeasing him or her? *Always* ask your Dom when in doubt." He moved over to her desk and said in a subdued voice, "By the way, Miss Wilson, you must raise your hand and wait to be called on in this class. Another such outburst will not be tolerated."

Brie smiled, enjoying her rival being properly chastised in front of the class. Mr. Gallant frowned. "And you, Miss Bennett, must learn to keep your feelings to yourself."

She was sure the other girls were silently laughing at her expense.

Hell, I deserve it, she thought, appreciating the irony of the situation. "I'm sorry, Mr. Gallant. It won't happen again."

He accepted her apology with a curt nod and added, "You should be supporting and learning from one another during the next six weeks. Anything less is a waste of this valuable opportunity. Have I made myself clear?"

Brie thought it was unfair that he was picking on her when Blonde Nemesis was the real problem. However, she took his reprimand to heart and bowed her head. "I understand."

He said kindly, "Miss Bennett, when you are in my class you will look me in the eye. I am your teacher and you are my student, no different than any other teacher you've had."

She raised her head and he gave her a hint of a smile. Then he turned to the rest of the class. "However, you are expected to behave quite differently outside this classroom. When you are in the presence of the other Dominants you do *not* make eye contact."

He'd said *other Dominants.* Did that mean he was a Dominant himself? She'd expected as much. What would it be like to be under the power of a man like that? She doubted he was sadistic, but he was certainly imposing despite his small stature.

Brie was thankful Mr. Gallant couldn't read her

mind. He continued the lesson without interruption. "Eyes will be kept downward at all times, unless you are being directly spoken to by the Dom in charge of you."

She started sweating. It would be far too easy to accidentally look into the eyes of other people. It was an ingrained habit of hers. She couldn't trust people unless she did. This new task might prove harder than walking in the damn shoes.

Mr. Gallant broke her train of thought with his commanding voice. "During your first practicum today, you will be working on proper body language. Every part of your body needs to express your submissiveness, things as simple as the placement of your arms and hands. I should not see anyone cross their arms or close their fists. Your lips should remain slightly open and supple at all times. Even the tilt of your head matters. Constantly ask yourself, 'Is my body communicating openness and willingness to please?' He pointed at each girl. "Why don't you check yourselves right now? Is your body open or closed? Adjust accordingly."

Brie noticed her legs were crossed, so she uncrossed them and sat up straight. She relaxed her mouth a little and put her hands on the desk in front of her. Mr. Gallant nodded towards her and then turned to the girl with perky boobs. "Ms. Taylor, you must sit up straight at all times. Slouching is a sign of disrespect."

The girl blushed and sat up quickly.

"Miss Sanders, even if your eyes are down, you should always turn your head towards your Dom or trainer so he or she knows you are being attentive."

The tiny brunette had been looking at the cuticles on

her right hand. She put her hands in her lap and answered, "Sorry, Mr. Gallant."

He moved on to Blondie. "Miss Wilson, you look like a proper submissive." She dropped her eyes down and gave a self-satisfied smile. "Except for that just now. A smile at the floor can be interpreted as defiance."

"Yes, Mr. Gallant."

"Class, as submissives you are poetry in motion. Every movement you make should be graceful and alluring—whether you are kneeling before your Dom or doing the dishes. However, any movement to draw attention to yourself is unacceptable, such as sticking your chest out to show off your breasts or even tossing your hair. It shows a lack of modesty and control."

Sanders raised her hand and waited to be called on. "But wouldn't our Doms want that?"

"Your Dom expects you to follow his orders to the letter. Controlling your movements signifies to him, and everyone else in the room, that you respect his leadership."

"I guess that makes sense," she mumbled.

"Even the words you use are of extreme importance. It is common practice for submissives to answer in a positive manner, even when indicating no. An example of a negative response would be, 'No, Sir, only if it pleases you'. Such an answer lets your Dom know your preference, but allows him to make the final decision. If you want to answer affirmatively, say, 'Yes, Sir' or 'If it pleases you, Sir'. If you feel neutral, a good answer would be, 'As you say, Sir'."

"What if he does something you don't want?" Taylor

asked. Mr. Gallant stared at her until she meekly raised her hand.

"Yes, Ms. Taylor?"

She slouched in her chair out of shame and repeated the question.

The man was not amused. "Are you trying to insult me on purpose?"

Ms. Taylor looked stunned and shook her head.

"Then sit up."

Blonde Nemesis let out a snicker. The glare Mr. Gallant shot her rival sent shivers down Brie's spine. She hoped never to see that look directed at her.

He answered Taylor as if nothing had happened, once she was sitting properly. "It is common to have established safety words, such as the colors red, yellow and green to indicate comfort level. However, if you have chosen well you should not have to worry about your Dom doing anything to harm you. Yes, he may push your limits in order to help you grow, but a good Dominant cares about the well-being of his sub."

Out of the blue, Mr. Gallant addressed Brie. "Did you do your assignment?"

She wanted to shrink away in embarrassment with Blondie watching, but she looked him in the eye and answered, "Yes."

"Please demonstrate."

Brie stood up gracefully and immediately felt the pain of being in the six-inch heels all day. Her mouth puckered in distress, but she didn't make a sound.

"Lips," he commanded.

She relaxed her mouth by opening it slightly. Brie

walked around the room, concentrating on the click of the high heels to distract her from the anguish. She looked in his direction and was disappointed that he wore no expression on his face—positive or negative.

"Sit back down."

Brie did so gratefully, assuming no reprimand meant she had done well enough. She hid the extreme relief she felt at getting off her throbbing feet. If she had been alone, she would have thrown the painful shoes across the room and rubbed her aching toes.

Mr. Gallant addressed the class as a whole. "Your first practicum of the night is about to begin. You are expected to follow the common etiquette we discussed here in class. They will judge each of you on how well you adhere to what you've learned. Proceed to room twelve and make me proud."

A new room meant new adventures! The thought made Brie giddy and overrode the pain of the shoes. She felt as if she were walking on clouds as she made her way to Sir.

Choosing to Obey

Brie glided into room twelve, hoping to see Sir. Just like on the first night, the trainers were sitting at a table in the front of the class. The room itself looked like a dance studio, with its smooth wooden floor and its walls lined with mirrors. The only thing missing was a handrail for ballerinas. At the table sat her four trainers: the bodybuilder on the far end, the ghostlike man with the penetrating eyes in the middle alongside the severe-looking Dominatrix, and Sir.

Before they advanced into the room, Sir commanded the girls take off their shoes. Brie saw him glance towards her, so she quickly averted her eyes. Brie kept them down, but it was difficult when all she wanted to do was drink in his presence. She stood silently, double-checking that her body was communicating openness.

"Ms. Taylor, you are slouching unattractively," Sir announced.

Out of the corner of her eye, Brie saw the young woman stand up straighter. "Sorry, Sir."

"Be aware of yourself at all times. Remember, there

are four of us watching you carefully." He stood up from the table and walked over to the students. Brie remembered to follow him with the turn of her head while still looking down.

"You will be practicing movement today. The mirrors are here to aid you in finding the most graceful ways to kneel, present, and rest. For now, I want you to lay your shoes by the door and line up in front of the panel."

They quickly did his bidding, lining themselves up in a row before the trainers. She noticed Sir standing next to Blonde Nemesis. "Show me, Miss Wilson, how you would kneel."

The other girls watched from under hooded eyes as Blondie knelt down. Her hands were open and loose at her sides, but her legs were spread apart seductively, showing off her crotch. Was she trying to flirt with him?

"I am not your Dom and we are in a public setting. This is not appropriate."

Sir moved over to Brie. "Kneel."

She knelt down slowly with her hands at her sides, open and relaxed. She kept her legs closed and her back straight. Even though the position was not exactly comfortable, she remembered to keep her mouth relaxed.

"Put your arms behind your back," he commanded.

She did so, but did not stick out her chest overly much, trying to keep a modest pose.

"Class, look at Miss Bennett. This is an appropriate stance. Kneel similarly."

The three other women knelt before the trainers with

their hands behind their backs. Brie glanced in the mirror, liking the way she looked.

"Clasp your hands behind your necks," he ordered. They all followed his instruction. "Ms. Taylor, you are slouching again." Once the girl had readjusted, he told them, "Now, hands at your sides."

He walked past each of the women and stopped at Miss Sanders. "Your hands look awkward. Look in the mirror to see what I mean."

Sanders repositioned her hands after checking herself. "Much better," he complimented.

Brie craved his attention and wanted him to return to her.

"I want you to turn towards a mirror and try out the various kneeling positions until you find one that feels most comfortable and sensual to you."

Brie was disappointed when Sir went back to his seat, but she turned towards the mirror and practiced kneeling. She eventually decided sitting on her calves with her hands behind her back was the most pleasant position for her.

Ms. Clark, the Dominatrix, spoke up. "Decide on a stance and take it now."

The girls faced the trainers again, with eyes still averted, and got into proper kneeling positions.

"Fine. Keep those positions until we return in a half-hour." One of the girls gasped and Ms. Clark snapped back, "Not another sound from any of you. Do not move until we return."

The four trainers walked out of the room.

Brie hated seeing Sir leave; it was as if he had taken a

part of her with him. Kneeling on the hard floor with the other girls was not what she had expected. However, she was determined to impress the trainers by obeying their command perfectly.

She closed her eyes and daydreamed about Sir touching her. His warm hands caressed her breasts and pulled at her hard nipples. Then they made a leisurely trip down between her legs. Sir unapologetically explored her depths with his fingers. Brie opened her legs wider for him, denying him nothing even when his fingers sought out her tight little asshole. She held her breath as he pushed two fingers inside. It hurt, but she didn't protest because she wanted more of him. He groaned in satisfaction as he replaced his fingers with the head of his cock, bracing himself to thrust. "Are you ready to please me?"

"Kneeling hurts," Taylor said, interrupting her delicious daydream.

"Shh…" Sanders cautioned.

"No, really. I thought we were going to have fun. I was looking forward to more wild sex. I didn't sign up for floor sitting."

Brie suddenly wondered if there were cameras hidden in the room. Could the trainers see and hear them? Regardless, she was going to pretend Sir was watching her right now. He would expect her to obey to the letter. She closed her eyes again and tried to ignore Taylor when she started cracking jokes.

"Hey, Bennett, you know you are a submissive when you wish your MasterCard would give you orders."

Blonde Nemesis laughed aloud and Brie was sorely tempted to join her, but she swallowed several times and kept silent. She chose to think instead of being whipped by Sir for her disobedience. The more she thought about it, however, the more she wondered if she'd like it. The way Sanders had enjoyed her whipping the day before made Brie think it might not be unpleasant.

By the time the trainers returned, the room was quiet again. "You may stand," Ms. Clark announced.

Taylor scrambled up, groaning loudly. Brie concentrated on trying to move gracefully even though her body was stiff. She stumbled a little, but got to her feet.

The ghostly white trainer stood up and addressed the girls. "Look me in the eye and tell me if you obeyed the command."

Blondie spoke first. "Yes, Marquis Gray."

Sanders was next in line and answered, "I did, Marquis Gray."

Brie wondered what Taylor would say, but the girl remained silent.

Brie looked into Marquis' intense eyes and almost lost her power of speech. It was as if he was looking into her soul, wanting to devour her. "I did as you commanded, Master." She blanched a little and corrected herself. "Marquis Gray."

He snorted. "You may call me Master if you wish." There seemed so much more behind his words than a simple jest. It made her quiver inside.

Blondie tattled shamelessly. "Marquis Gray, Taylor did not follow your command."

He glanced Blondie's way, but did not acknowledge her. Instead, he looked at Ms. Taylor and asked, "Is this true?"

She responded immediately, "Yes, Marquis Gray."

"What did you fail to obey?"

"I talked, sir."

"Is that all?"

Blondie spoke up again. "She made jokes and complained. She tried to ruin it for the rest of us."

Marquis Gray's eyes narrowed as he glared at Taylor. "I do not think you are worthy of our training."

Brie didn't want to see Taylor go; she really liked the girl's sense of humor. "Marquis Gray, do I have permission to speak?"

He walked over to her and moved in invasively close. Brie's nostrils were assaulted by his manly scent and she felt the heat of his breath on her cheek. "Speak," he commanded.

"Ms. Taylor was trying to...keep our spirits up. I do not feel she should be punished for trying to help."

"Should you be punished then?" he asked in a deep, ominous tone.

She quickly answered in the negative. "Only if it pleases you."

He leaned in next to her ear and whispered hoarsely, "Ah, but it would please me..."

Brie felt her insides contract in fear. Marquis Gray moved back to the table and the four trainers discussed the situation quietly amongst themselves.

Had Brie just ruined her chance with Sir by standing up for Taylor? She had to fight off the tears burning her eyes. She was determined to remain strong and take the punishment with dignity. Taylor glanced her way with an apologetic look in her eye. Blondie, however, gloated.

Brie wanted to wring her thin, little neck.

Sir stood up. He smiled pleasantly at her nemesis and stated, "I will speak with you privately, Miss Wilson, following the practicum."

Brie's heart fell. Had he chosen a new favorite based on her actions?

Marquis Gray addressed Taylor. "Your disobedience must be punished, regardless of the reasons for it. You will be joining me at the end of the practicum."

Neither trainer spoke to Brie. They continued the practicum with no further explanation. Master Coen, the overly muscular trainer, snapped his fingers. Four attractive men entered the room and stood before each of the girls. Brie faced a gorgeous man with long, dark bangs that partially covered his eyes. He had a sexy Asian look to him that reminded Brie of her favorite character in Japanese anime. His features were definitely pleasing, but all she could think about was Sir.

Master Coen addressed the group. "Your Doms will be teaching you basic positions. We will be observing how well you respond to their instruction. Expect to be critiqued afterwards." He sat back down, picked up a pen and began scribbling something. She wondered which of them had already screwed up.

Brie closed her eyes and was instantly hit with a vision of Sir taking Blondie in his office. It tore at her heart. Then her Dom commanded, "Look at me." She opened her eyes and gazed into the richest chocolate brown eyes she'd ever seen.

"You will address me as Tono." His voice had a velvety quality that thrilled her.

"Yes, Tono."

During his instruction, Tono's hands moved constantly over her skin, correcting, caressing, and teasing her. Brie kept taking quick glances at his magnetic eyes, captivated by them. He caught her several times but did not correct her.

Tono carefully instructed her on how to 'kneel up' and 'kneel down', what stance to take while at 'rest', and the kneeling position he preferred in a private setting. "Spread your legs in a tempting V for me and clasp your hands tightly behind your back so that I can enjoy those beautiful breasts." When she did, he lightly grazed her nipples through the corset and her whole body tingled with sexual tension.

His final lesson was on how she should 'present' herself to him. "I need you on your hands and knees, back arched, chest forward, head down, legs spread far apart so everything is displayed for my pleasure."

Just his description made her loins wet. She followed his instructions, but he nudged her legs out even farther and told her to arch her back more. The position was uncomfortable, but she had no doubt the view he had was revealing. She took a quick glance in the mirror. The line of her body reminded her of a cat in heat.

His hands caressed her ass underneath the skirt and then moved up her back to her hair. He grabbed at a handful of her brown curls and pulled her head back to kiss her. "You learn well, toriko."

Ms. Clark ordered the girls to undress and kneel beside their Doms. Brie tried to remain graceful as she undid her corset and shimmied out of her skirt. She slowly unrolled her hose and stepped out of them. Brie walked over to Tono and knelt down sensually. She was desperate to see the look on Sir's face, to know if he was displeased with her. However, she kept her eyes down and waited for her next instruction.

Sir stayed at the table, but addressed the girls individually. It was another round of humiliating critiques. None of them was spared, including Brie. Ms. Clark seemed especially disgusted with her. "Are you aware that you interacted with your Dom as if he was your intimate lover and not your superior? You were constantly looking him in the eye."

Brie nodded her head once in acknowledgment. Master Coen spoke next. "You must remember your place, Miss Bennett. I believe your Dom was being overly lenient with you today. I also noticed you were stiff in your movements. Practice your transitions."

Marquis Gray's voice was smooth and dangerous. "You seem to have a power over your Doms that needs correction. I wouldn't want to see it crushed, as it is a part of your charm. However, it needs to be reined in."

Sir had only one comment. "Go home tonight and practice your transitions, as Master Coen suggested."

"It will be my pleasure, Sir." She looked into his eyes, hoping for a sign of approval, but his expression was nondescript.

He ordered, "Class, you will now present yourselves to your Doms and please them as they see fit."

Brie hid her disappointment and immediately dropped to the floor. "Not here," Tono said. He held out his hand and helped her up. "Move over to the mirror. I want you to watch me enjoy your body." She allowed him to guide her and waited for his first command.

"Present yourself to me," he said huskily. She got into position, straining to arch her back in a beautiful curved shape with her legs spread, just as he had instructed. She kept her head down, waiting for his next order.

Brie heard him undress and her loins burned with desire. There was something intoxicating about this Dom. It was obvious he had been handpicked for her based on the questionnaire she had filled out, but it was more than just his looks. She felt a deeper connection.

Tono positioned himself behind her and then commanded, "Look in the mirror."

She lifted her head and looked into the reflection. His eyes radiated fiery lust, making her moan softly. He heard it and smiled. "Yes, let me hear your pleasure."

Brie purred, "Yes, Tono."

He grabbed her hair and pulled it back as he rubbed his hard shaft against her swollen pussy. Watching this beautiful man about to mount her was more than she could take. Her passionate cry echoed through the room when he held her waist and penetrated her. Tono's cock was thick, giving her a satisfying sense of being filled. He plunged deeper into her willing depths. She moaned for him, loving the way he stroked her with his manhood.

Tono leaned forward and murmured, "Look me in the eye, my little sex slave."

This Dom knew Brie's desire and wanted her to get lost in his gaze. She stared into those gorgeous brown eyes as he took pleasure in her body, his thrusts hard and demanding.

"Toriko, you have the prettiest honey-colored eyes." He added lustfully, "And I like the way your tits bounce with each thrust of my cock."

She asked, not wanting to break his command, "May I look, Tono?"

"I want you to."

She looked down at her dancing breasts. With each hard stroke, they bounced delightfully. It gave her a sense of power to know her breasts heightened his enjoyment. She gazed into his eyes again and smiled—her smile just for him. Tono was intoxicating.

"I shall plant my seed deep inside you, toriko." She moaned loudly, wanting to feel his come bathe her insides. He took both hands and grabbed her buttocks, commanding that she arch her back farther, keeping her eyes on him as he came.

Then Tono released his passionate wrath on her body. She couldn't breathe as he rammed her with his shaft. It was amazing and frightening, the way he owned her with his cock. She never broke eye contact with her Dom. She knew the moment he released his seed inside her and her entire body hummed with pleasure.

"Thank you, Tono, thank you…" she whispered.

He slowed down, but remained inside her. He looked at her in the mirror, commanding something with his eyes that he did not voice. Suddenly, the delayed contractions of a sweet orgasm took her and she caressed his manhood with her climax. Wetness flowed from inside her depths, spilling out when he disengaged from her.

"That's my good love slave," he said, petting her long hair. "Now clean it up with your panties." She did so immediately, embarrassed to have made a mess. He took the thong from her and kissed it. "This, I keep."

Both dressed quietly while the others finished with their sessions. Before he left, she knelt beside him and bowed. "Thank you, Tono."

He told her to lift her head up and then said softly, so only she could hear, "I will be back for you."

She smiled at him affectionately. "If it pleases you."

When he left, she turned in the direction of the four trainers. She kept her head bowed in the respectful kneeling position she preferred. After all the men had left, Sir spoke to the class. "Those who have not been called to meet privately will proceed to the commons. Someone will come to get you for the second practicum."

Brie watched poor Taylor follow the silent and foreboding Marquis out of the room. She could see Taylor shaking. How bad would her punishment be? At least the girl always had the option to quit if it got too rough.

Sir nodded to Blonde Nemesis and only said one word. "Follow."

Brie watched helplessly as Sir left with her. To keep herself from falling apart, she reflected on Tono's lovemaking. Even if Sir no longer wanted her, at least she had a Dom she adored.

Facing the Unknown

B rie and Sanders proceeded to the commons and found a lovely salad and some wine set out for them. The two sat down and began eating quietly. "What's your first name?" Brie asked between bites.

"Teri."

Brie held out her hand. "Well, hello, Teri. My name is Brie."

Teri took her hand and shook it firmly. "Pleasure to make your acquaintance. Hey, do you think Taylor will be okay?"

"I have to believe the school wouldn't be world re-nowned if they abused their students."

"I know, but man, I wouldn't want to be her right now. That was brave of you to stick up for her like you did."

"I just hated how Blondie—I mean, Wilson—tattled on her. Especially after Mr. Gallant instructed us to support each other."

"Yeah, I don't trust that woman farther than I can throw her. I can't believe she is getting special treatment from Sir for being a rat."

Teri couldn't have known how her words would affect Brie. She suddenly imagined Sir mounting Blondie as they spoke, and it made her blood run ice cold. "Oh well, eventually she'll get hers," she grumbled.

They were finishing their meal when Taylor walked in. Her eyeliner was smeared on her cheeks as if she'd been crying, but she seemed peaceful. She sat down next to them and started to eat.

"Are you okay?" Brie asked.

She looked up from her food and nodded. Then she went back to eating in silence.

"Are you planning on staying in the program?" Teri asked.

Again, she looked up and nodded, but didn't speak.

Brie decided to ask her a question that could not be answered with a simple yes or no. "So, my name is Brie and this is Teri. What's your name?"

Taylor smiled and started playing with her food instead of answering them. Brie looked over at Teri and shrugged.

Taylor pushed her plate over, and Brie saw that she had spelled out the name 'Lea' in green beans.

"Your name is Lea?" Brie asked.

She nodded and took the plate back, stabbing the green beans and eating them with gusto.

"I guess she isn't allowed to talk as part of her punishment," Teri commented.

"Yep, that's a safe bet," Brie agreed. She patted Lea on the back. "I'm glad you're staying with us. I enjoy your jokes."

Lea's eyes sparkled. Brie could tell they were going to be good friends.

Soon after, Blonde Nemesis joined them. She, too, was quiet. Brie examined her, trying to discern whether she had coupled with Sir or not, but Blondie's face was unreadable. The girl picked up her plate and moved to another table to eat. Her lack of gloating spoke volumes.

Master Coen eventually came to the commons to direct them to the second practicum. If Sir was planning to dominate her tonight, this would be when he'd do it. The end of the second night was fast approaching.

The girls walked into the auditorium and sat at the front, just as they had the night before. Sir did not waste any time. "As with last night's practicum, we want you to observe and learn from your classmates. There is no point in repeating a lesson when you are perfectly capable of learning from each other."

Marquis Gray stood up and called out, "Miss Wilson, you will be our first tonight."

She nodded in his direction, looking a bit sheepish. Then she gracefully walked up the stairs to the stage and turned towards the little group. Her eyes rested on Brie. There was an unmistakable look of hatred in them. *Good.* Sir had not shown her any 'special treatment'. Brie smiled back at her sweetly.

Marquis Gray stated, "Miss Wilson, last night you faced an activity you claimed to dislike with a Dom that you did not find attractive. Tonight, the same partner will join you on the stage to help you experience some-thing unknown. We want to see how you adapt to new situations and to what level you trust your Dom."

Brie was confused. It did not seem that Sir was going to take her after all. It robbed her of the joy she'd been carrying all day. She struggled not to pout as she watched Blondie get her wrists bound to her ankles and then be gagged by her Dom, a man who resembled a scrawny computer nerd. It looked extremely uncomfortable, but the girl never once lost her look of serenity. Blondie responded to her Dom's caresses, groaning in pleasure when he took off her thong and started playing with her pussy. "Don't move," he commanded.

He began by teasing her with his fingers, tongue…and teeth. She gave a muffled cry when he thrust his fingers deep into her pussy. It was obvious from her abundant juices that she was enjoying his attention. He finally released the gag and commanded that she suck him dry. She eagerly latched on to his thin cock and sucked with fervor.

He had complete control over her because her wrists were bound to her ankles. He thrust his shaft repeatedly into her mouth, ordering her to take it deep. She moaned in pleasure, apparently enjoying his rough treatment.

Brie assumed he would come in her mouth, but he abruptly stopped and left the stage for a couple of seconds. He returned with a large purple dildo and told her to spread her legs farther. He slowly inserted it into her vagina, and then the air filled with the distinct sound of humming. Blondie whimpered in pleasure, obviously enjoying the vibrations of the toy.

He thrust his cock back into her mouth and started pumping away. "I want you to come when I do." Blondie looked up at her Dom in lustful adoration. It didn't take long before he tensed and shouted, "Come for your Master!"

Blondie clamped down on the dildo between her legs and started groaning as he came in her mouth. The excess of his ejaculation dripped down her chin. Brie felt a gush of wetness between her own legs. Why she was getting horny watching Blondie orgasm was beyond her, but what made it even worse was that she didn't have panties on. Tono had taken off with them. She shifted uncomfortably, realizing she had just made the seat slippery with her juices.

Blondie thanked her Dom after she was unbound, and walked unsteadily back to her seat, weak from the sexual encounter. Sir stood up and spoke. "That was enjoyable to watch, Miss Wilson. I take it you were pleased by the scene your Dom set up?" Blondie nodded. "Well done."

Sir then looked at Brie. "What is your problem, Miss Bennett?"

She wanted to curl up and die, but she answered him clearly. "I have made the seat moist, Sir. I have no underwear."

Brie saw a smile tug at his lips. "Is that because you enjoyed the scene?"

"Yes, Sir."

"Very good."

From out of nowhere, an assistant came up and handed her a small towel. She tried not to think about everyone watching her as she cleaned off the vinyl seat. She sat on the towel, to prevent any more issues. Brie stared straight ahead and ignored Blondie's barely audible laughter.

"Ms. Taylor, please join your partner on the stage," Marquis Gray announced. Lea walked onto the stage and met her Dom, a large, roly-poly man. Brie watched as he undressed her, exposing her recent punishment for all to see. Lea had red welts on her buttocks. Brie was surprised when Lea glanced quickly in Marquis' direction and smiled. *Did she enjoy her punishment?*

Sir called her on it. "Ms. Taylor, all smiles should be directed at your Dom and no one else." She bowed to Sir, and then turned to her Dom and bowed.

He accepted her silent apology and directed her to lie on the mat he had laid out. A table stocked with items had been produced between scenes. He picked up a long red candle and a box of matches from it.

He knelt beside her and with slow precision, he lit the candle and watched it burn. Once it started dripping wax, he commanded, "Arch your back."

Taylor arched her back beautifully, thrusting her chest in the air. He tilted the candle over her right breast and let the hot wax run onto her nipple. Brie noticed that she jumped, but Lea did not make a sound. The liquid wax slowly traveled down her round breast to her ribcage and onto the mat.

Her massive Dom switched to the left breast and let the wax drip onto that nipple as well. She jumped again, making Brie wonder just how hot the wax was. He stood up and retrieved another candle. "I want to see you pleasure yourself with it."

Lea took it from him and slid it between her legs. She rubbed it against her pussy as he continued to tease her with the hot wax. Lea inserted the tip of the candle inside herself and lifted her hips up. She started pumping it into herself and her Dom growled in satisfaction.

He dripped the wax over her stomach, causing her to squirm further. Then he pulled his cock from his briefs and demanded she stroke it. She continued to thrust the candle deep as she stroked his shaft with her other hand.

He dribbled the wax over her mound and Brie heard Lea take a sharp breath, but otherwise remain silent. "You like it, don't you, pet?" he crooned over her. Lea nodded.

The massive man moved between her legs and took hold of the candle she was playing with. He pulled it out and placed it on the stage floor. He replaced the candle with his substantial cock. Lea wrapped her legs around the man's great waist and threw her head back in what looked like pleasure. It was odd to watch the scene play out without her vocalizations, which helped reinforce the lesson Brie had learned the night before. She definitely needed to communicate effectively with her Doms.

He dripped the candle onto Lea's pussy, covering it, and his cock, with the wax. He groaned in pleasure and did it again before blowing out the candle. He braced himself and then started ramming his dick into her. It was oddly fascinating to watch the body fat of the man move in waves as he pounded her fiercely.

Other than short gasps, nothing escaped Lea's lips. Only his cries of passion echoed in the auditorium. He clutched her and finished with solid thrusts. Brie didn't know how Lea had stayed silent through her pounding.

After he had pulled out, he leaned down and handed

Lea a new candle. "I want you to come," he said in a hoarse voice.

Lea grabbed it and began stroking herself with the same rapid pace her Dom had used when he'd fucked her. He rubbed her clit relentlessly with his beefy fingers. Soon Lea's hips were convulsing in a rhythmic motion. Still, no sound came from her lips. Brie was impressed. Whatever Marquis Gray had done must have had a profound impact on her. Lea was doing everything in her power to stay in the program, and Brie was pleased.

Lea bowed to her Dom afterwards and quickly got dressed. She sat down, positively glowing. It was obvious she had enjoyed herself. Brie leaned over and whispered, "I thought of a joke for you."

Lea looked at her and smiled encouragingly.

"A masochist begs a sadist, 'Please hurt me.' The sadist looks over with an evil smile and answers, 'No.'"

Lea turned a deep shade of red and swallowed several times, trying not to laugh. For a second, Brie was afraid she was going to break her silence. Instead, she patted Brie's hand in appreciation.

Yep, we're going to be good friends.

Sir addressed the class again. "Ms. Taylor, you showed excellent control. I am glad to see you taking your lessons seriously. You followed your Dom's lead and enjoyed yourself in the process. Is that a fair assessment?"

Lea nodded her head.

"Excellent. Then we shall move on."

Brie's heart was beating rapidly. There were only two girls left, and once she stepped onto the stage she would finally know if Sir planned to be her partner. Unfortunately, Marquis Gray called out Sanders' name next.

"Good luck," Brie whispered to Teri as she got up from her chair. Her hairy partner stood on the stage, waiting for her. Sanders' Dom was a giant teddy bear of a man, all fur and muscle. Brie noticed that she paused on the stairs before continuing up.

The Dom had been tender with Teri after their little whipping lesson on the first night. It was obvious he had feelings for her. Unfortunately, it was equally obvious those feelings were not returned by the tiny brunette.

This time he was not carrying a whip. Instead, he was holding what looked like a delicate chain. Brie couldn't begin to guess what he was planning to do with it. "Take off your top and put your hands behind your neck."

Again, Teri hesitated. She slowly removed her corset and let it fall to the floor. She looked over at Sir before taking a deep breath. Teri clasped her hands behind her neck. He tied them together with a simple black ribbon. The pose looked quite sensual to Brie.

"Do you know what these are?" he asked in a deep baritone.

Teri shook her head.

"These are nipple clamps. They have a bit of a bite to them."

He went to caress her breast with his large hand, but she shook her head. "No...I mean, red."

Marquis Gray spoke up. "Miss Sanders, are you refusing the lesson?"

"Yes."

"May I ask why?"

"I felt all confused after last night's whipping. I liked it at the time, but later I didn't. I don't care for the feeling of not being in control."

Master Coen conferred with Sir before stating, "We think it would be best if you ended the program now. Either you are not ready, or this is not your calling."

Teri shifted uncomfortably. "Yes, I don't think this is for me."

Her Dom untied the ribbon and Teri grabbed her corset and rushed off the stage. Brie was brokenhearted that she was leaving. Sir's claim that someone would quit the program was coming true, but Brie had never expected it would be Teri.

"Please don't leave us," Brie begged.

Teri shook her head as she quickly dressed. "I can't do this, but best of luck to you two," she said, purposely ignoring Blondie.

She looked over at the trainers. "Thank you. I've learned a lot from this experience."

They inclined their heads towards her in response, and Sir added, "If you ever change your mind, our doors are open to you."

She turned and walked away, the auditorium reverberating with the sound of her clicking heels.

It was a lonely sound.

Learning to Trust

B rie could tell Sir was looking straight at her, but she kept her eyes down. Now was her moment of truth. "Miss Bennett, come up to the stage."

She glanced up at him and basked in his warm smile, but her heart skipped a beat when he went to sit back down. She slowly walked up, her disappointment hard to mask. When she saw Baron walking up the other side, she gasped. His look frightened her.

Baron wore a black leather mask over his head. It covered his entire face and gave him an ominous quality. It instantly brought up her childhood memories of being beaten in school. She started to back away as he approached. "Don't move," he commanded.

It wasn't until she looked into his eyes that she stopped shaking. Baron's dark hazel eyes reflected confidence in himself and in her. She stared into them, trying to regain her courage.

Ms. Clark protested, "Miss Bennett is doing it again. She is not averting her eyes as a submissive should."

Brie instantly looked down, but trembled as he

moved towards her. When he placed his dark hand on her forearm, she was instantly transported back to her childhood. She whimpered pitifully, "Don't hurt me."

Baron lifted her chin and looked directly into her eyes. "You are going to have to trust me."

The connection was re-established and her fears began to abate. He ran his hands over her body, reminding her of his gentle caress. He was not one of the bullies of her past, even if he looked dangerous behind that dark mask.

Ms. Clark interjected, "If she looks you in the eyes when you are not speaking to her, I want you to punish the girl." The word *punish* only added to Brie's blossoming fear. She tried to calm her breathing, knowing that she was close to hyperventilating. She heard Baron growl under his breath. His negative response to Ms. Clark's order reassured Brie, and she began to relax. She could trust him. He would not do anything to harm her.

A strange rope contraption began to lower from the ceiling. Brie tensed when she saw it.

"Have you ever tried a sex swing before?" Baron asked.

She shook her head, glancing at him only briefly before looking down again. The mask really upset her.

"It is not the only surprise I have for you, kitten."

Brie felt her pulse begin to race. He slowly undressed her, and then placed his dark hand over her left breast. "Your heart is beating so fast," he murmured, nuzzling her neck. She longed for him to kiss her, but the leather mask prevented it. It was an unwanted barrier between them.

Baron lifted Brie off her feet effortlessly and placed her in the swing, directing her to put her feet in the hanging stirrups. It had almost a bondage vibe to it that she liked. "Use your hands to support yourself like on a regular swing," he instructed, letting her go. She swung slightly in midair. It was a completely helpless feeling to have her pussy open and splayed out for her Dom's taking.

He disappeared from her line of sight while she swung there. She tried to ignore the fact the other girls could see her most intimate parts. Baron had a knack for exposing her to the audience like that. It made her wonder if he did it on purpose.

When he approached her again, she suddenly panicked. The dark mask, his dark skin, and the aggressive way he moved towards Brie reminded her again of the beatings she had taken when she was young. She started whimpering and struggled in the harness, desperate to get away from the pain she knew was coming.

"Shh…" he said softly. She looked into his eyes and instantly knew calm. She could trust him as long as she was connected to him through his gaze. He moved between her legs with an unknown object in his hand and she did not struggle.

Ms. Clark stood up to protest, but Sir intervened. "Baron knows what he is doing. Let him train his sub without interruption."

Brie felt Baron spread a watery gel over her clit and outer lips. Immediately, she felt heat begin to build on the affected areas. She didn't know what it was and started panting in distress. The burning continued, growing even stronger.

He left her again. When he returned, he slipped a ring over his cock and moved over to her head. "Pleasure my dick," he ordered.

She leaned her head back and opened her lips wide to take in his shaft. He guided her movements and she swung back and forth, taking more and more of him with each pass. His manhood responded to her attention and grew considerably in girth and length.

"Do you feel the heat?" he growled seductively. She nodded an affirmative with his cock in her mouth. "It is going to enhance your experience, kitten. I plan to torture you with pleasure."

Brie moaned. The words 'torture' and 'pleasure' didn't belong in the same sentence, but she was curious as to what it meant for her.

He pulled away and commanded, "Head back." She pulled her head back farther and looked down at the stage floor. He let her swing there for a few moments. The waiting, not knowing what he had planned, was torture in itself.

She felt him move between her legs and then he lightly stroked her clit. The gel he had applied made her super sensitive. She gasped in surprise and pleasure. In just a few minutes with only the lightest of touches, Baron had her orgasming for him.

He chuckled softly. "I let you have the first one for free, but now you have to wait until I give you permission to come."

"Yes, Baron," she answered, unsure how she was going to control herself.

He grabbed her thighs and eased his cock into her moist tunnel. He pushed her away from him and then pulled her back. The swing added force to the movement and her pussy crashed against his cock, sending pleasant shockwaves through her. Brie squealed in excitement.

"You like, that don't you, sex kitten?" She nodded, trying to ignore the throbbing pleasure between her legs.

He increased the force of his thrusts, making her clit ache with need. Whatever he had lathered on her was having a major effect. She whimpered, each thrust sending fire-bursts of pleasure through her.

"Feeling good? Well, I am about to send you over the edge. Don't you dare come."

She bit her lip as he started manually playing with her clit while penetrating her. Brie started whimpering and then screaming as she felt her pussy contract. There was no stopping it, and she came all over his cock.

Baron tsked and pulled out. "Now you must be punished."

Instead of fear, her poor pussy contracted in pleasure. It wanted whatever attention he planned to give her. He walked off the stage and returned with a flogger. It looked like a whip, but with many angry tails. She shuddered and closed her eyes, waiting for her punishment.

"Open your eyes and tell me what you did wrong."

Brie looked at him warily and answered, "I came without permission."

"Yes. As a responsible Dom, it is my duty and privilege to punish you. Lean back and lift your legs higher."

Brie did so, knowing that she was giving him free

access to whip her bare bottom with the wicked-looking flogger. She soon felt the multiple tails of the whip slap across her buttocks. She jumped at the impact, yelping from the sting.

Then he left her. She couldn't tell where he went, but she was suddenly alone on the stage, swinging gently in the air. It was a horrible feeling. Not only had she disappointed him and the whole room knew it, but it was that much worse knowing he was gone. She ached for him to return and had to fight off the tears as she slowly swung back and forth. The room was deathly silent.

Although it was probably only minutes, it felt like hours before she heard his footsteps on the stairs. "Are you ready to obey me?" he asked.

Brie looked at him in desperation. "Yes, Baron. I want to obey you."

He began caressing her clit and instantly sent her back to the pleasurable fire she'd felt before. The only thing that kept her from giving in to it was knowing that she would lose his presence again if she did. She moaned and squirmed, but she did not come. He slipped his cock back into her pussy and started fucking her with passion. She denied herself, wanting to please him more than to experience her own release.

"Do you want to come, kitten?"

"If it pleases you, Baron."

"Good answer…but not yet."

Baron took full advantage of the swing, pulling all the way out and then letting her swing right back onto his hard rod. The explosive jolts from each impact threatened to overcome her resolve to obey him. Finally, he grabbed onto her hips and began quick, hard thrusts. She felt his cock grow thicker just before he came. "Now," he gasped between ejaculations. She closed her eyes and allowed the intense throbbing to morph into pleasurable contractions. Brie cried out as the chills took hold and she lost touch with reality.

Baron's warm chuckles brought her back. He had already pulled out and was standing beside her. "That was a good effort, my sweet little sex kitten." He picked her up and helped her out of the swing. As soon as her feet touched the ground, the swing rose back up into the ceiling.

Brie had to hold onto him, needing time to get her legs back. "Thank you, Baron," she whispered. He ripped off his mask and bent down to kiss her with those thick, warm lips.

She struggled to get her clothes back on, and then turned to Sir and the other trainers.

"What did you learn, Miss Bennett?" Sir asked.

"That I don't want to disappoint my Dom."

"Good."

Ms. Clark stood up, obviously still unhappy. "The next time I see you staring into the eyes of your Dom when it is not appropriate, I will punish you myself."

"Yes, Mistress Clark," Brie answered.

The hostile trainer seemed to appreciate the title Brie had given her, and her expression softened a little. She sat down without another word.

Brie left the stage and walked over to her seat. Instead of lecturing them further, Marquis Gray handed out paper and told them to write down what they had learned from their fellow classmates. She was the last one to finish. When she had handed in her paper to Marquis Gray, Sir dismissed the group. The second night of training was officially over.

She felt a profound sense of loss, knowing that Sir did not want her. She got up slowly and groaned. Her feet were on fire, protesting vehemently against the torturous shoes. With gritty determination, she walked gracefully towards the auditorium door. Just as she touched the latch Sir said, "Miss Bennett, proceed to room two."

Brie almost squealed like a little girl, but somehow kept her composure. She said loudly, "Yes, Sir!" and disappeared through the door before she could make a fool of herself.

The Power of *His* Touch

B rie walked down to room two, no longer concerned about her aching feet. She tried to open the door but found it locked. She stood there alone with her eyes directed at the floor, waiting for Sir to join her. *Be still my heart*, she repeated to herself, many times over. It seemed like an eternity before she heard his footsteps coming down the corridor—long, confident strides.

Sir did not acknowledge her, but went to unlock the door. As he entered the room, he said quietly, "Follow."

Brie immediately moved behind him, and then gasped when she saw the interior of the room. There was the same table with leather straps that she'd seen on the website. That picture of it had convinced her to start the submissive training in the first place.

"How did you know?" she whispered.

"Know what, Miss Bennett?"

"That I wanted this."

Sir laughed lightly. "The way you responded to Miss Wilson's lesson today made it fairly obvious." She was embarrassed, but grateful he could easily read her desires.

He pointed towards two chairs in the corner. "I want to talk to you before we begin."

She nodded, and sat down only after Sir took a seat.

"Miss Bennett, you should know that I am breaking protocol here. Normally, a trainer does not interact with a student, but I am not a man who is easily denied. I have wanted to take your sweet little ass ever since I saw you bend over the box of cigarettes in the tobacco shop. As headmaster of this school, I know where your training is headed and if I want your anal virginity, I need to take it now."

His words sent shivers of delight through her body. "I understand, Sir."

"You can refuse me."

"I do not wish to, Sir."

"Fine. Then undress and kneel beside me."

Brie forced herself to breathe normally as she slowly and sensually took off her clothes for him. She folded them in a neat pile and then knelt down beside her Sir. He began stroking her hair, making her purr inside.

"I saw how you handled yourself after we left the room earlier. I was pleased with your obedience." Brie had *known* there were cameras. "I appreciated that you stood up for Ms. Taylor."

Brie looked up and smiled at him. "Thank you, Sir."

"Although I agree with Ms. Clark that you have an eye contact issue, I understood your need for it in the auditorium with Baron." He glanced down at her with a glint in his eye. "I enjoyed watching you train with him tonight." He continued to play with her hair and her whole body tingled with bliss. "I have a question for you, however."

She looked deep into his eyes. Whatever he wanted to know was his for the asking. "What, Sir?"

"Tell me, what did Tono say to you at the end of your first session today?"

"He said that he would come back for me."

"Hmm…" Sir rubbed his chin thoughtfully and was silent for a moment. "It appears he, as well as another Dom, is infatuated with you. After we finish here, I want you to follow me to my office. There is something I need to give you, Miss Bennett."

Before she could respond, Sir pulled her head back and kissed her roughly. All reasoning left her when she felt his insistent lips on hers.

He picked her up in one swift motion and carried her to the table. He strapped her wrists down first, leaving no room for movement. Before he secured her ankles, he took one of her feet gently in his hand. "I see those shoes are doing a number on your pretty little feet. Does it hurt?"

"Not much," she lied.

He smiled and lightly caressed them. "My devoted little student," he murmured. Then he secured her ankles so that her legs were spread and ready for him.

Sir walked to the other side of the room and opened a door. She heard the sound of running water. When he came back, he had a wet cloth in his hand. He used it to tenderly bathe her entire body. Every time the cloth began to get cold, he went back to the room and rinsed it with warm water. By the time he was finished, she felt completely clean and fresh.

He put the cloth away and shut the door quietly. Instead of coming to her, he leaned against the wall and stared at Brie—at her naked body, strapped down and eager for him. She basked in his gaze. It was just like the website photo; her fantasies were now her reality.

"Some men think they need toys to excite a woman, but I don't believe that. No, I believe firmly in the power of touch." He continued to gaze at Brie, without making a move towards her. The fact he was taking his time made her want him all the more.

When Sir finally pushed away from the wall and walked towards her, she was literally trembling in anticipation. When his hand lightly touched her stomach, she gasped. All her awareness was focused on that one area. He gave her a leisurely smile as his fingers made their way up to her breasts. Brie closed her eyes when they made contact with her hard nipples. She moaned without meaning to and heard his light chuckle.

"That's it, Brie. Give in to your desire."

Hearing Sir call her by her given name affected her deeply. She began panting, unsure if she could handle his lovemaking.

He bent over her and began sucking on her left nipple. She bit her lip, trying not to cry out like a silly girl. Sir pinched her other nipple and then started sucking harder. She arched her back in response, moaning his name.

He reached one of his hands between her legs and felt her excitement. "You're one hot, little sub," he murmured seductively. "Something tells me your body is aching for me to fuck your sweet, virginal ass."

Brie whimpered and rubbed her eager pussy against his hand. He penetrated her moist depths with his middle finger. "Hot and willing, are you?" Sir pulled his finger out of her wet pussy and then pressed his tongue against her throbbing clit. He started licking the sensitive nodule as he pushed his slippery finger against her anus. She cried out passionately as he pushed his finger into her nasty little hole.

"Oh, this virgin may be tight, but she wants my cock stroking her in the ass," he said confidently. She nodded in agreement, too embarrassed to agree with him out loud.

Sir would have none of it. "What does this little virgin want?"

Brie paused a few seconds before answering. "To be taken by you, Sir."

"Beg for it, Brie."

"Please, Sir. Take my virginal ass with your cock."

"Do you want me to be gentle or rough?"

Again, she paused. "Whatever is your pleasure, Sir."

"So agreeable, like a proper submissive," he growled. "I think it pleases me to give you both…"

He quickly undid the restraints and told her to get on her hands and knees. He strapped down her wrists so that she rested her weight on her forearms. Then he buckled her ankles in place, leaving her with her legs spread apart and her ass in the air.

With unhurried motions, Sir undressed in front of her, exposing his manly chest first. It was covered in dark hair and well-defined muscles. She watched with desperate interest as he unbuttoned his pants and pulled them off, along with his briefs. His cock was princely, perfectly proportioned with a thick base and a slightly longer than normal shaft.

"Oh, yes. This entire cock is going deep inside you today," he assured her.

Sir moved onto the table and positioned himself behind her. He caressed her round buttocks, squeezing them in his hands before lightly slapping each. "There is nothing sweeter than a virginal ass begging to be fucked. Tell me again what you want, Brie."

"I want you deep inside me, Sir."

"As you wish."

She suddenly felt cold gel drip into the crease of her buttocks, and then Sir's finger pushed the cool liquid into her warm, puckered hole. He soon replaced his probing finger with his sizable cock. He wasted little time forcing the head of his shaft into her. Brie gasped and panted as she grew used to the new sensation. Even after the butt plug the day before, she found his cock stretching her in places never tried before. It almost hurt, but her body needed him so badly.

"Relax, Brie. Let my cock dominate you," he murmured, stroking her hair. Sir reached around and began caressing her breasts as he groaned passionately in her ear. Centimeter by centimeter, Sir made his way into her tight, virginal hole. He opened her up more the deeper he pushed. "We're halfway, Brie. Do you think you can take more?"

She didn't know how, but she wanted more and answered, "All of you, Sir."

He grabbed her waist and began thrusting, slowly

and sensually. The concentrated movement relaxed her tight muscles and he finally pushed his entire cock into her resistant depths. She moaned at the sensation of fullness his thick cock gave her.

"Now that I have given it to you gently, I think it is time I switched gears."

She whimpered, despite her hungering desire for him.

"I want to hear your unrestrained cries when I fuck your little ass. Don't hold anything back."

"Yes, my Sir."

"*My* Sir—now that's a little presumptuous of you, isn't it?" he chuckled, before giving a quick and hearty thrust into her ass. Brie squealed at the intensity of it. "Would you like another?" he asked.

She nodded her head enthusiastically, but said nothing.

"No, Brie, you must voice your desire."

"Please, Sir, may I have another?"

The instant the words left her mouth, his cock thrust deep and true. She cried out, surprised at the depth of his penetration. "Now, Brie. Would you like me to fuck your sexy little ass?"

"If it pleases you, Sir."

She felt his hand tighten around her waist while she waited for his pounding. Sir's thrusts became hard and commanding. She started to moan and then cried out, holding nothing back as his hard shaft stroked the inside of her tight hole.

Sir's groans of pleasure were music to her ears. To please her Sir was Brie's deepest desire, so when his fingers entered her wet pussy and he ordered her to orgasm, she released all her pent-up passion and came violently around his fingers.

His surprised groan sent a second wave of pleasure crashing over her. As if he couldn't take it, he immediately grabbed her hips and began stroking into her ass for all he was worth. She reveled in it, loving every second of his passionate pounding. She screamed out his name when he stiffened inside her and began bathing her ass with his hot seed. *There is no greater joy than this!*

When Sir finally pulled out of her, he seemed more vulnerable, more approachable. She longed to be released from her bonds so that she could wrap her arms around him and kiss him all over. Instead, he turned away and got dressed.

When Sir came back to her side, he was once again the authoritative headmaster. He undid her straps and ordered her to get dressed. Brie had to move slowly, still shaking from the heated exchange.

"Don't put your shoes on yet," he told her.

After she was fully dressed, he called her to kneel beside him. He stroked her long hair in such a loving manner. It made her wish she could remain beside him like this forever. Eventually, he ordered her to stand up. She did so gracefully, desiring to please him. She desperately wanted to gaze into his eyes, and silently begged him to speak to her.

She was pleasantly surprised when he pulled her against him and lifted her chin up. Sir's lips pressed against her mouth and she moaned in pure ecstasy.

"Something tells me that this ex-virgin would like

more."

"Yes, Sir," she purred.

"Too bad, my dear. You must wait."

She wanted to seduce him, but remembered her place. "As you please, Sir."

She stepped into the torturous six-inch heels and hid her pain with a look of contentment. She followed close behind Sir as he walked down the hall, curious to know what he planned to give her.

As soon as they entered his office, he commanded her to kneel again. He sat down at his desk and began searching through the bottom drawer. He held up a thin black collar. Brie's heart wanted to burst with joy. It was obvious he wasn't pleased with the other Doms showing an interest in her, and she'd read online that a collar was a sign of ownership.

"As one of my students, you are under my charge. I cannot have Doms endeavoring to claim you before the course is finished. There is still much for you to learn." He walked back over to her. "Brie, it would be foolish to choose a Dominant until you have more experience. Although I can safely say that all of the Dominants used in training would make good partners, I do not want any of them attempting to sway your decision. Therefore, I am placing this collar of protection around your neck."

She felt his manly touch as he fastened the collar on her. Brie closed her eyes, her stomach fluttering at the intimate contact.

Sir continued, "This will be a visual reminder for others to keep their distance until your training is complete." He said in a lower voice, "This does not indicate my ownership of you."

Brie's heart dropped, but she said, "Thank you, Sir."

He chuckled lightly. "Everything you feel is written on your face, Brie."

She felt shame and then wanted to die because he could tell. Sir lifted her chin. "I am your trainer. I cannot claim you as my submissive." He kissed her one last time, and the collar around her neck rubbed pleasantly against her delicate skin.

It didn't matter that Sir had said to wait until her training was over. In this one area, Brie could not obey—her heart was already his.

An Exchange of Gifts

The sun streamed into her bedroom, announcing the start of a new day. Brie curled up under her blankets with a grin on her face as she relived her encounter with Sir. His erotic touch had surpassed her wildest dreams and she could not forget the look of vulnerability on his face afterwards. She knew he felt the strong connection, but Brie had to be patient. As her trainer, Sir was not allowed to claim her.

Still... She caressed the thin black leather collar around her neck. He insisted it was a 'protection' collar so the other Doms would not influence her during training. She had a sneaking suspicion the collar's true purpose was to stake his unspoken claim on her. Brie didn't mind; she wanted Sir all to herself.

She popped out of bed when the alarm started beeping. Today would be her third day at the Submissive Training Center. Of the six women who'd started the program, three had already dropped out. The first two sessions had been meant to weed out wannabe subs. It made her wonder what tonight's training would be like, now that only serious submissives remained. She trembled with excitement.

Brie dressed for work, this time choosing tight-fitting jeans, a black silk shirt and her six-inch heels. After only a few days of class, she already looked at herself in an entirely new light. She'd always worn clothes for comfort, but now she wore them for power—sexual power. It was thrilling to observe the positive reactions from men, and sometimes even women, in the confines of the little tobacco shop.

People treated her differently now. Mr. Reynolds, who had always been respectful, now treated her with reverence. It was intoxicating. Even Jeff, who was worthless as a coworker, tried to get in her good graces. He stocked the cigarettes on his own these days and pointed it out, hoping to impress her.

Um…that's his job, she thought as she priced the new shipment of tobacco. When the door to the little shop opened, she looked up, wondering which of their regulars it would be. Her stomach did a little flip when she saw it was Tono. He looked at her with those rich, chocolate brown eyes and a smile that melted her heart. Seeing him in her work environment was disconcerting, but in a delightful, earthmoving way.

She stood up slowly and faced him, practicing her grace and poise. His eyes traveled from her face to her neck, but then locked on the collar. Without a word, he turned and left the shop.

She felt the urge to run after him, but stayed where she was. She fingered the thin, leather protector around her neck. *Who knew it had that kind of power?*

Brie was grateful Sir had thought to collar her. She would never have guessed that Tono would be so quick to start something outside the Training Center. Sir had read the Dominant's intentions well. It was obvious that the young Dom respected Sir, based on his quick retreat.

However, something pricked her consciousness. Even though she was devoted to Sir, there was no denying she had feelings for Tono. She couldn't shake the feeling of disappointment at not getting the chance to talk to him. She hoped she would see the charming Dom that evening, so that she could express with her hands what she had been unable to say with her mouth.

After work, she readied herself for class, taking special care with her nails. She painted them a deep red, wanting them to look as sexy and desirable as her lips. Once she was dressed in her corseted school uniform, she practiced her transitions from a kneeling position to standing in front of her full-length mirror. *Beauty and grace*, she repeated to herself.

She was so caught up in doing it perfectly that she forgot the time. Brie had to grab her long coat and rush out of the door. When she got to the campus, she only had four minutes to make it to class. She turned her ankle, smashing hard into one of the business students at the entrance of the school. He caught her in his arms, preventing her from falling onto the cement.

"Whoa, where's the fire?" he asked with a smooth chuckle.

She looked up into crystal blue eyes and forgot herself for a second. She shook her head. "I'm sorry, I have to go or I'll be late."

She whipped off her shoes and ran for the elevator. With seconds to spare, she made it to the classroom and sat down at her desk. She gracefully slipped her heels back on just as the bell rang.

She glanced up and saw everyone staring at her. Brie smiled innocently and shrugged. Mr. Gallant began his lesson on cue, not allowing her dramatic entrance to disrupt his teaching. She wondered if he would reprimand her after class.

"It is important that you understand the power you have as a submissive. It is not a case of you being inferior when you bow at your Dom's feet. The reality is your Dom only has the illusion of power. You are the one in control. You decide how far the scene will go. It is your gift to him or her. The Dominants in this establishment understand this and treat it as the valuable gift it is. Not all Doms are as enlightened, but we will talk about that another day."

He walked from the other side of the room to Brie's desk. He glanced at her collar momentarily and then began speaking again.

"You will find the more power you give up, the more powerful you will feel. You are, in essence, giving a magnificent and selfless gift to your Dom. It is sacred. Never lose sight of that. A true submissive is a jewel of great worth." His voice dropped lower and became sensual when he added, "There is nothing more intoxicating than looking down at my sub when she's trembling at my feet in breathless anticipation for my next action or command." Brie found her body responding to his words and had to force herself not to envision herself bowing at his feet.

He continued, "What does your Dom give back to you? He takes on the responsibility of caring for your needs throughout the scene, but he also brings to the table his imagination and experience. His is the art of arousal. A Dominant's job is to increase his submissive's state of excitement throughout the encounter, while at the same time testing and challenging her limits. Not an easy task, mind you, but one well worth the staging and planning required." Mr. Gallant's voice took on a silky consistency. "The union of a dedicated Dom and a confident submissive is a harmonious marriage of souls. There is no other experience like it."

Brie closed her eyes as he spoke, his words resonating through her. Just listening to his description of a Dom/sub relationship gave her chills of pleasure. She couldn't wait for the next practicum.

"I would like you to write down a favorite scenario that arouses you. One you have fantasized about for years because it makes your loins quiver when you think about it." He handed out cloth-covered notebooks, each one different. Brie's was a luxurious wine color. "This is your fantasy journal."

She opened the book and was delighted to see each page was lined with gold. It was an opulent book, made to hold her sumptuous and naughty dreams. Mr. Gallant then handed each of them a gold pen. "You will not find a better writing instrument."

Brie took hers and wrote her name on the first page. The pen glided over the paper effortlessly. She purred, loving everything about this assignment.

"Please include as many details as you can," he continued. "You will also want to describe your feelings throughout the fantasy. You will find it aids tremendously in understanding your deepest desires. Being an exceptional submissive depends on you connecting to your unspoken needs and underlying motivations. A fantasy journal can help you do that." Mr. Gallant sat down at his desk and proceeded to write in his own journal.

Since she was a filmmaker, Brie's fantasies were complicated affairs. They had to make sense and her characters needed to have believable backstories or she couldn't get into it. She took a deep breath and dived in, knowing exactly which fantasy she wanted to release onto the page.

My parents wanted to move us to Kansas in the hope that we could make a fresh start. My father had been a dreamer ever since I could remember. He'd lost everything we'd owned pursuing his impractical schemes. It didn't surprise me when he jumped at the chance of free land when they opened up the West. He had no qualms about taking his family into the wildness. When I voiced my innate fear of Indians, Papa chastised me so severely that I never spoke of it again.

I was only eighteen at the time, a proper young woman of marrying age. Naturally, my mother and I were concerned about finding a suitable husband for me on the prairie. Papa dismissed those worries as well, claiming that Kansas men came from good stock and I would have plenty of fine gentlemen to choose from.

We were just days from our destination when our wagon train came under attack.

I hear the wild cries before I see them circle us. A cold chill grips my heart. Momma screams, "Run, Isabella! Run as fast as you can!" She pushes me off the wagon. The terror I feel gives my feet incredible speed. I don't look back when I hear her scream—I only run faster.

I sprint until my sides ache, but I refuse to stop, knowing that it will spell my doom. Just when I think I can run no more, I come upon a stream and plunge my face into the cool water, to try to quench my insatiable thirst.

After several desperate gulps, I feel eyes boring down on me. I look up to see a savage warrior on a roan horse. He says nothing, watching me from the other side of the stream.

His look is foreign and frightening: bronze skin, long black hair, high cheekbones, and eyes that pierce my soul. When his horse starts towards me, I spring in the opposite direction even though I know it's pointless. In a matter of seconds, the horse is running beside me.

The Indian launches himself off the large beast and tackles me to the ground. I struggle beneath him, but I am powerless against his incredible strength. He chuckles, as if he enjoys my terror. Then he turns me over in the dirt and crushes my body with his weight while pulling my hands above my head. I look into his dark eyes and see unbridled lust. It both frightens and excites me.

His lips come down on mine, demanding and firm. I whimper softly, unable to break from the intimate embrace. His smell and taste assault my senses, stirring something inside me I haven't felt before.

Suddenly, he lifts himself off and ties my wrists together with a leather strap. He boosts me onto his horse and gracefully jumps on behind me. He nudges the magnificent beast towards his village. Once we arrive, I see that his people are celebrating the raid and showing off the spoils. As horrifying as that is, I cry out in panic when a brutal-looking warrior pulls me from the horse and drags me away.

He is stopped and a verbal exchange begins that I do not understand. To my relief, my original captor leads me to his tepee, but then he leaves me there alone. I listen to their inhuman screams and laughter throughout the long night.

Eventually, he enters the tent. I am petrified. Tears stream down my face unhindered, for I know he is about to take me. My only consolation is that he is not the other warrior. He gently wipes the wetness from my cheeks and murmurs something reassuring I can't decipher.

I stiffen when he forces me down onto the buffalo hide. I feel his hands reach under my dress and I cry out for mercy. There will be no mercy tonight. I close my eyes tightly when he forces my clenched legs apart.

He moves between them, his manhood pressed against my womanly flower. I start to scream, but his lips muffle my cry. I struggle at the burning, pinching sensation caused by him forcing his large shaft into me. When he has pushed the entirety of his cock into my virginal depths, he stops and gazes into my eyes. There is something tender in the fierce eyes of my warrior.

He kisses me again and I feel myself start to melt. I am his now.

He gives a deep, guttural growl before he begins stroking me with his rock-hard...

"Please place your journals on my desk."

Brie looked up with a frown, disappointed that she could not finish the fantasy. Glancing around, she noticed that the other girls had finished. Brie wondered if she was the only one who entertained such detailed fantasies. She lovingly fingered the book before placing it on Mr. Gallant's desk. Sitting back in her seat, she willed her body to calm down. It was only a silly fantasy, after all.

"Before you start your practicum tonight, I want to inform you of tomorrow's event. We started our first class on Wednesday for a reason. We wanted two days to weed out the non-submissives and one day to prepare you for the auction."

Now he had Brie's full attention.

"Every Saturday, you will participate in a private auction. It provides you with a chance to practice what you've learned while experiencing different Doms outside the Training Center. Rest assured, the Dominants invited to these auctions are prescreened. We guarantee whoever ends up 'winning' you for the day is worthy of your trust."

Brie's heart rate shot up. *An auction?* Her loins warmed at the thought of being purchased by a stranger and used for the day. Even though she was certain it wasn't a possibility, she daydreamed Sir would be the one to win her.

"Tonight's practicums have been especially designed to meet your individual needs. We want you prepared for tomorrow's event. Take what you learn to heart and trust our training methods." For some reason, Mr. Gallant stared directly at Brie when he said it, making her curious about what lay ahead.

As she was leaving the classroom, she heard him call out her name and her heart sank. "May I have a word with you?"

He was going to lecture her about almost being late—she just knew it. Brie walked over to him sheepishly. Mr. Gallant didn't need to reprimand her; there was no way she would make that mistake again. Her ankle was still aching from when she'd wrenched it.

"I have a quick question," he said kindly. She smiled, feeling a surge of relief that he wasn't going to chew her out. "Why are you wearing a collar?"

Brie blushed slightly when she explained, "Sir felt a few Dominants needed a visual reminder to stay away until the end of the course."

"Interesting," he said, as if to himself. "Thank you, Miss Bennett. You may leave."

She hurried towards the door, excited to join the others for the first practicum. Before she made it out of the room, however, he added, "For the record, being late is a sign of disrespect."

She cringed inside, but turned and gave him a bright smile. "I promise not to let it happen again, Mr. Gallant."

She almost threw him a kiss goodbye because she was so giddy about the upcoming session, but managed to stop herself. *OMG, how embarrassing would that have been?*

Blind and Stripped

They entered room twelve again, the room that looked like a dance studio with its mirrors and wooden floors. Brie remembered to take off her heels and to keep her eyes down when she entered. She stood before the panel of four trainers, trying to suppress the smile that threatened to spread across her lips. Being in Sir's presence after such intimate contact the night before gave her delicious butterflies.

"Tonight's first practicum will involve yesterday's Doms putting you through your paces. We want the commands to be second nature for you, but we also expect to see grace and poise at all times," Sir explained in his deep, commanding voice. Brie physically trembled at the sound of it.

Their handsome Doms entered the room—all except Tono. Instead of her gorgeous Dom, Brie had a small Middle Eastern woman. Had Sir ordered Tono away because of his interest in her? The thought both saddened and pleased her.

Ms. Clark stood up and walked over to Brie. "Miss

Bennett, because you had such difficulty averting your eyes yesterday, you will wear this the entire night." She produced a blindfold and ordered Brie to turn.

Brie swallowed hard. Facing the unknown without the benefit of sight was terrifying to her. "Please, Mistress Clark," she begged, "I learned my lesson, I promise." However, she made the mistake of looking directly in Ms. Clark's eyes.

"Turn," barked the trainer angrily.

Brie dutifully turned. With deft movements, the imposing Dominatrix tied on the blindfold and snorted. "I am a strict teacher, Miss Bennett. You will learn that I do not tolerate disobedience."

In a softer tone, Ms. Clark said, "Let me know if she disobeys you in any way."

Brie heard a gentle voice answer, "Yes, Mistress."

"You may go now."

Brie felt a tight grip on her arm as the tiny woman led her from the room. Everything in her cried out to remain with Sir, but she knew defying Ms. Clark was not an option. Obviously, as the headmaster of the school, Sir agreed with her punishment or he would have prevented it.

She tried to hide her disappointment by concentrating on the woman's touch. Although it was tight, the woman exuded calm control. Brie remembered Mr. Gallant's assertion that she should trust the trainers' lessons tonight and forced herself to relax. *This is to prepare me for the auction,* she repeated to herself.

She felt a temperature difference in the new room they entered. It was significantly colder, which made her

Teach Me: Brie's Submission

nipples harden into tight buds.

"I want you to undress and lie on the table," the woman commanded softly as she directed Brie's hand to the edge of it.

Brie ran her hands over the table to get her bearings before undressing. She left her clothes on the floor and climbed onto the small table. It was barely wide or long enough to hold her. She gasped when her warm skin touched the cold vinyl. Then she heard the distinctive sound of stirrups being pulled out from the table, as if she were at a doctor's office. With small, warm hands, the woman placed her feet into them.

It reminded her too much of a medical exam. "Please, Mistress, what are you planning to do?"

"I am not a Mistress. I would have you call me Sting, but I do not want you to speak again. Nod if you understand."

Brie nodded, trying not to let her fear take over. Why would this woman be called Sting?

She heard a buzz and felt the woman touch her mound. "Don't move."

Brie bit her lip, tensing up until she felt the pleasant vibration of an electric razor. The woman trimmed her pubic hair with quick motions. Afterwards, she smelled the sweet scent of talcum powder as Sting sprinkled it over her mound and rubbed it into the skin.

Brie heard her leave the table and move across the room. When the woman returned, she felt the edges of a tray as it was placed between her legs. She tensed again, making Sting laugh. "Relax, Miss Bennett. I am good at what I do."

111

Good at what?

Brie suddenly understood when she felt the hot wax. The woman pressed a strip of cloth against it and—without any warning—ripped it clean off. Brie screamed in surprise and pain.

"No more noises from you," the woman admonished.

Brie swallowed hard as Sting spread the second application onto an adjacent area and pressed another strip of cloth onto the wax. When the woman readied for the pull, Brie held her breath and then screamed silently, feeling each individual hair rip from her body as the woman yanked off the wax. An errant tear slid down her cheek.

"Good girl," Sting replied soothingly. "If you breathe in when I pull, it won't hurt as much. However, I recommend you give in to the pain. Some of my clients come when I do this."

Brie couldn't imagine that and had to squelch another shriek. Sting was relentless as she plucked at the remaining hairs. She could only imagine what her now completely bald nether regions looked like. Afterwards, Sting applied a soothing cream to her burning skin.

"You did well, Miss Bennett. I will report that to Mistress."

The fact that Sting had simply called her Mistress made Brie think she was Ms. Clark's official sub. Brie had so many questions she wanted to ask Sting, but obediently kept silent.

Once Sting had cleaned up the room, she took Brie by the arm and helped her off the table. Brie stumbled, still recovering from the shock of the treatment.

"Take your time to dress," the small woman said gently.

With shaking hands, Brie pulled on her crotchless hose and then attempted to tie her corset. After several failed attempts, she felt Sting take over. She tied it far tighter than Brie ever had. So tight, in fact, that she had trouble breathing.

"There. You look much better now. You should strive to always keep it this tight." She helped Brie into her skirt and shoes. "Hold your panties in your hand. Mistress will want to examine my work."

Brie blanched at the thought, but nodded. Sting led her back to the main room, where she heard the grunts and moans of the couples finishing their sessions together. Brie sighed inwardly, unhappy that she'd had to endure pain *and* miss out on a sexual encounter. Ms. Clark definitely knew how to make a punishment hurt on many different levels.

Brie stood there quietly until she heard the Doms leave the room.

Ms. Clark spoke in a firm voice. "Was she obedient?"

"Yes, Mistress."

"Fine. Let me see."

Brie felt the hem of her short skirt being lifted up. For the first time that night, she was grateful for the blindfold. It was humiliating to be treated in such a manner. She could only imagine the delight Blonde Nemesis must be experiencing at witnessing her degradation.

"Well done," Sir complimented. Brie's whole attitude

changed with his simple statement. If her new look pleased Sir, then there was no reason to feel mortified.

"Attractive," Marquis Gray added. His voice held a possessive tone that unsettled Brie.

"Enough about this girl's kootch," Master Coen said. "We need to discuss the next practicum."

Ms. Clark spoke up. "You may go now, pet. Thank you for your service."

"It was my pleasure, Mistress." Then Sting whispered to Brie, "Hold onto me while you put your panties on."

Brie leaned against her as she tried—as gracefully as possible—to follow her command, despite the tight corset, high heels and blindfold. Blonde Nemesis snickered softly, so that only Brie could hear.

After Sting had left, Brie heard manly footsteps enter the room and wondered who it was. Sir addressed the group. "You will proceed to the commons. Miss Wilson, you are responsible for escorting Miss Bennett to and from the commons tonight."

Brie groaned inside, but dutifully followed Blonde Nemesis. As they walked down the hallway, Wilson laughed. "Nice kootch, Bennett."

"Shut up. You're just jealous," Lea retorted. She grabbed Brie, and the three walked arm in arm as if they were all good friends.

"What do you think this practicum is going to be like?" Brie asked. "It seems odd that they are still talking about it."

"It does make me suspicious, especially with Mr. Gallant joining them," Blonde Nemesis said.

Brie was curious now. *All five trainers are discussing the next practicum?*

"I really don't care," Lea replied. "So far, I have enjoyed everything we've done except that whole kneeling test." She giggled pleasantly. "Thank goodness I can talk today. By the way, Wilson, what *is* your first name?"

"Why should I tell you?"

Brie turned to her even though she couldn't see. "Because, like it or not, we're in this together."

"Whatever."

Lea pressed, "So, your name *is…*?"

"Mary."

"Oh, like the Virgin Mary?" Lea teased.

"Shut up, Lea Fake Boobs." Mary immediately turned on Brie. "So, what happened last night?"

Brie chose not to answer. Lea nudged her playfully and asked, "What's Mary talking about, Brie?"

Mary answered for her. "She didn't come out with us. I waited for more than a half-hour, but she never came out of the school."

"What kind of weirdo are you, stalking me like that?" Brie asked irritably.

"Don't avoid the question, Bennett. Don't think we haven't noticed that collar around your neck," she replied, jealousy tainting her harsh voice.

"Oh, Brie, tell me what happened last night," Lea begged.

She wasn't about to share her intimate moment with Nemesis around. "Sir was concerned that one of the Doms was getting too attached, so he gave me a protection collar."

Mary breathed an audible sigh of relief. "Okay, if it's

just a protection collar it means nothing."

"Which Dom is it?" Lea wanted to know.

"Tono," Mary answered.

Brie growled angrily, "What's wrong with you, Wilson? Lea asked *me* the question, not you."

"But I am right, aren't I?"

Brie said nothing, angry that her nemesis knew so much. When they arrived at the commons, Brie could smell a variety of spicy foods. "What is it?" she asked.

"All kinds of tasty Spanish tapas!" Lea squealed. "I'll make us both a plate," she said, and left Mary to lead Brie to a table.

"Don't get used to this, Bennett. I can't stand you," Mary hissed. She left, presumably to get her own plate. Brie didn't mind if she was jealous—she didn't mind one bit.

It surprised Brie how much better the food tasted with her blindfold on. She noticed every little nuance of flavor: garlic, spicy cayenne, sweet paprika, the honey-bitterness of saffron. The same went for the wine, with its layers of smoky cherry and vanilla, as well as a hint of oak. She let the other two chat away as she enjoyed the aromatic food and partook liberally of the multilayered wine.

Master Coen did not come to get them for a full hour. By then, the mutual excitement of the three was deliciously tangible. They walked arm in arm to the auditorium, trusting that the practicum was going to be out of this world.

Challenged

Once Brie had sat down in the auditorium, Ms. Clark ordered her to take off her blindfold. She did so quickly, blinking several times to adjust to the light. "I expect you to observe everything, Miss Bennett. Do *not* look away."

Brie thought it was an odd thing to command, considering all of the girls were expected to watch, but she nodded and looked towards the stage dutifully.

Master Coen spoke to the group. "Tonight is a special night for each of you. This is a night of self-discovery, where we promise to stretch your limits and open you to desires you've avoided up to this point."

Brie was dumbfounded when she saw Ms. Clark move onto the stage. Master Coen announced, "Ms. Taylor, join your trainer."

Lea looked at Brie, her eyes wide with curiosity. She bounced up the stairs and joined their Dominatrix trainer with the severe bun and tight-fitting business suit. "For this exercise, you will address me as Mistress," Ms. Clark ordered.

"Yes, Mistress," Lea said, her gaze glued to the ground. Obviously, she didn't want to suffer the same punishment as Brie.

"Am I correct in assuming you have not been with another woman?"

"Yes, Mistress."

"Then your name for the scene shall be Cherry. Take off your top and underwear, but do it thoughtfully. Please your Mistress as you reveal your large bosom and your cunny to her."

Lea slowly undid the ties of the corset and playfully uncovered one of her unnaturally large breasts. She covered it back up and exposed the other before letting the corset fall to the stage floor. She turned away from Mistress Clark and flipped her skirt up. Then she bent over and slowly shimmied off the thong, stepping out of it and spreading her legs.

"That was nice. Now stand up and face me, with your arms crossed above your head." Lea readily obeyed her command. Mistress reached over and cupped Lea's right breast in her hand. "A full D-cup—not too big, but more than a handful." She flicked Lea's nipple with her thumb, making it taut and erect. Then she moved her fingers to the other, tugging and kneading her breast. "Retrieve the nipple clamps from the table."

Lea glanced down at the small table and looked confused. She hesitantly picked up a small chain, then handed it to her Domme while keeping her eyes averted. "Yes, Cherry, those are nipple clamps. I take it you haven't tried them before."

"No, Mistress."

"Then we are both in for a treat." She opened a clamp and attached it to Lea's nipple, adjusting it until her sub grunted in discomfort. "Does it hurt, Cherry?"

"Yes, Mistress."

Mistress Clark adjusted it a little tighter before she moved to the other nipple. Brie cringed in empathy for her pain. The nipple clamps looked pretty with the decorative chain connecting them, but the idea of having one's nipples squished like that seemed extremely painful—as bad as waxing.

"Concentrate on the pain, don't avoid it," Lea's Domme insisted. Lea nodded and said nothing. When her face relaxed, Mistress Clark pulled on the chain. Lea moaned softly. "That's it. You feel the pleasure, don't you?" With her hand still pulling on the chain, Mistress Clark leaned over and kissed Lea, running her tongue over her lips before darting in.

Lea kissed her back, whimpering softly. She spread her legs open when Mistress Clark moved her fingers between Lea's thighs to caress her glistening pussy. Brie was shocked that their trainer could be so hot and provocative. It forced her to look at the woman in a completely different light.

Mistress Clark pulled back and put one of her legs onto the small table, hiking up her pencil skirt. "Cherry, I want you to eat my pussy the way you would like to be eaten."

Lea got down on her knees and moved the red panties aside so she could lick Mistress Clark's sex. Brie's eyes opened wide—it seemed so wrong and yet so erotic. Lea licked the length of it and then settled her tongue on the clit. The only sound in the entire auditorium was gentle suckling noises.

"Faster, Cherry."

Lea moved her head back and forth in a rapid motion, causing the Mistress to moan. Brie felt her juices start to flow at the sound of her trainer's pleasure. Never in a million years had she thought watching Ms. Clark would make her horny.

"Stop. That was good, Cherry, but I want you to stand up now."

Lea did as she was told, standing respectfully before her Mistress. The Domme picked up a fleshy-looking dildo and knelt down to partake of Lea. As she kissed Lea's drenched pussy lips, she pulled on the chain with one hand and thrust the phallus into Lea with the other. Brie could see that her friend was trembling from all the attention, and wondered how long Lea could last. The auditorium was filled with her panting moans.

"Let me please you, Mistress!" Lea begged.

"Yes, Cherry." Mistress Clark stood back up and kissed Lea on the lips.

Lea snuck her hand to Mistress' mound. The Dominatrix dropped the dildo and the two started flicking each other's clits like there was no tomorrow. The whole group waited in anticipation as the two women brought each other to climax. Lea was loud when she came, but only a few gasping sounds came out of the Domme's lips.

Brie's panties were sopping wet at the end of their encounter. It had been so simple, but Ms. Clark had known exactly how to play Lea. It had been like watching art—the art of seduction.

Master Coen asked, "How would you rate the scene, Ms. Taylor?"

She looked down and smiled, but then stopped herself. Lea was learning. She looked him directly in the eye before she smiled again. "I enjoyed it."

"Even though it was with a woman?"

"Yes, and it surprises me. I never would have guessed."

"Tonight's practicum was an important breakthrough for you," Sir commented.

She nodded enthusiastically. "Yes, Sir."

Once the stage was cleared, a new scene was set up. Assistants brought a bed onto the stage, along with a table and a single tube of lubricant. Brie started hyperventilating, thinking her time was at hand.

Her heart about stopped when both Master Coen *and* Sir walked up to the stage. Brie closed her eyes and waited for her name to be called.

"Miss Wilson, please join your trainers on the stage," Marquis Gray announced.

She stopped breathing altogether and her eyes immediately fell to the floor, but Ms. Clark was watching her. "Eyes on the stage, Miss Bennett!"

Brie obeyed. She did not miss the extra wiggle to Mary's ass as she walked up to the stage and stood next to *Brie's* Sir.

Master Coen commanded, "Slave, undress your Masters."

Mary deftly removed their clothes, starting with Coen first. The large muscular man was impressive without clothing. He had the look of a tanned bodybuilder, completely free of hair and with every muscle nicely defined. His shaft was already rigid. Like the rest of him, it was stout and veiny.

Mary was purposely slow and sensual when she undressed Sir. Her hands danced over his skin as she took off each piece of clothing. Brie had seen him *au naturel* before, but she was still surprised by how strikingly handsome he was. Unlike Master Coen, he had a covering of brown hair on his chest, arms and legs. His muscles weren't bulging like Master Coen's, but they were well defined and *fine*. Brie glanced between his legs, admiring his handsome cock surrounded by dark hair. She felt incredibly possessive of that shaft and didn't want Mary anywhere near it!

Sir murmured something, and Mary obediently got down on her knees. Brie wanted to close her eyes, but she resisted the urge and watched her nemesis go down on him, her stomach in knots. She *hated* Ms. Clark for making her watch.

While Mary continued to suck Sir's dick, Master Coen knelt behind her and began stimulating her clit with his hand. "Spread for me," he ordered. She obediently opened her legs wider and he pushed his fingers inside, pumping her deeply.

Brie's heart rate increased in both anger and desire. Why couldn't *she* have been the one up there? She felt a touch on her shoulder and knew it was Lea. Her friend understood, and knowing that helped Brie to check her building rage.

Both men disengaged from Mary at the same time.

Master Coen moved over to the bed and lay on his back. "Sit on my dick, slave. We're about to give you a ride."

Mary let out an excited squeal and climbed onto the bed. She straddled him, letting his veiny shaft impale her swollen pussy. Meanwhile, Sir took the lubricant and liberally coated his cock with it. Brie wanted to scream when he approached Mary. She gritted her teeth, willing herself not to look away.

Sir joined the two on the bed and spread more lubricant over the girl's tight hole. Mary moaned in anticipation. His velvety smooth voice explained, "I know this is your first time with double penetration, so we will take it slow initially."

"I want it, Sir," she groaned. "I want to please you."

"Of course you want to please us." He slapped her ass several times, the sound of it echoing through the auditorium. "Now relax and take it…" Sir said as he pushed the head of his shaft into her. Mary grunted as she received his gift.

Brie felt the weight of someone staring at her and glanced at the other trainers. Both trainers were looking at her, *not* at the stage. She quickly turned her eyes back to the scene, suddenly understanding that this was a test.

She watched as the men played with Mary's body, helping her to relax enough to take in the fullness of both of their cocks. It took several minutes before Sir's entirety was securely in her ass. Mary kept moaning, "Oh, God… Oh, God, that feels good."

Brie let out an irritated sigh. Even though she had only just lost her anal virginity the day before, she wanted to take Mary's place. *She* wanted to be the one pleasing Sir.

Mary let out a loud moan when Sir began moving inside her. Soon both men were alternately stroking her with their shafts. Their muscles strained as they controlled the depths and speeds of their thrusts.

It was incredibly erotic to watch a girl taking two men at the same time, but Brie was pissed. She didn't care for the scene, and wanted to close her eyes and ears to it. She tried to put herself in a 'happy' place, but that became impossible when Mary started screaming in pleasure. The men had increased their speed and Nemesis' body was responding favorably to it.

Sir slapped her ass hard. Mary's whole bodied stiffened before she cried, "Oh, God, *yes...*" and her buttocks began their rhythmic tensing. She moaned until the last wave of her orgasm had receded.

Both men reacted by pumping into her faster. Master Coen came first, with deep, low grunts like a wild boar's. Sir was silent, but Brie saw him stiffen just before his pelvis thrust rapidly against her ass.

Brie slumped lower in her chair, feeling defeated. Watching Sir come inside another woman was *too* much.

The three lay there in silence, gathering themselves, before Sir finally lifted himself off Nemesis, and offered his hand to her as she disengaged from Master Coen. An assistant quickly set a tray of towels on the table and retreated. Master Coen handed one to Mary so that she could clean herself.

Once she was dressed and the trainers had taken their seats, Ms. Clark spoke. "Miss Wilson, how would you rate this scene?"

"I give it a ten."

"May I ask why?"

Brie knew the real answer, but Mary replied, "Pleasing both men at the same time was amazing." She giggled and added, "I'd do it again right now." She kept her eyes to the floor, but Brie knew that her last answer was directed towards Sir.

Gloom descended over Brie when she realized who was left. Marquis Gray, the ghostlike man whose dark eyes could penetrate her soul. *He* was going to be her partner. The same man who had punished Lea by leaving red welts on her ass.

There was no way she was going to share a scene with that man. She stood up and started towards the door, walking away from it all—from Sir, from Lea, and from her submissive training.

Don't cry, she told herself.

Embracing Her Power

Lea reached a hand out. "Please, Brie. Don't go."

Mary chuckled under her breath as she sat down. *Yes, bitch, you win,* Brie growled silently.

She looked at Lea sadly and shook her head, unable to speak. She didn't want to go, but her stubbornness and pride refused to back down. She didn't even look at the trainers as she walked away. Her shoes made the same lonely clicking sounds Teri's had the night before.

"Brie…"

Sir's warm voice filled her senses, and she closed her eyes. His call was filled with gentle longing. Sir didn't want her to go. She stopped halfway to the exit and turned around.

Ms. Clark barked, "We did not give you permission to leave. Are you quitting the program, Miss Bennett?"

Brie looked her in the eye and said nothing. She looked over at Sir and thought she saw the muscle in his jaw twitch, but his face remained stoic. She looked at Master Coen next and noticed he had a self-satisfied air about him. When she looked at Marquis Gray, she felt a shiver of desire and fear. There was no doubt he wanted her, but he was at her mercy. She had the power to deny him—to deny them all.

What do I want?

She stood there and no one said a word, patiently waiting for her answer. Brie searched her heart. Yes, she wanted Sir more than any other man she'd ever known. However, if she was honest with herself, she wanted the training even more. With or without Sir, she *was* a submissive, and this was her opportunity to delve into all the possibilities that world afforded.

"I am not quitting the program," she announced.

"Then join your trainer on the stage," Ms. Clark said curtly, as if nothing had happened.

Both Marquis Gray and Brie walked up to the stage together. She involuntarily shivered when he put his hand on her shoulder and squeezed. Brie automatically glanced up and her blood froze.

"Miss Bennett!" Ms. Clark snapped.

She quickly looked down. The abyss of desire reflected in Marquis' eyes frightened her. She had to will herself not to run.

The bed from the last scene was gone. In its place was a small silver chest. "Undress for me, pearl." Brie thought it odd that he would give her such a pretty name, rather than 'slave' or 'pet'. She swept the thought aside and stripped gracefully for him. She was going to give them a show—all of them. She wanted everyone to know they hadn't broken her. No, in this moment she would be the most powerful sub on the planet.

"Turn and close your eyes," Marquis Gray commanded as he produced a ribbon of black lace. "I find lace far more attractive than traditional blindfolds."

A shiver went down her spine as he gently but securely tied the lace over her eyes. She could just imagine how sexy it looked.

He moved away from her, but soon returned, placing more ribbon in her hand. "It's black, like your blindfold. Feel it. I want you to envision what it looks like." She fingered the long, narrow length of ribbon. It was silky smooth, incredibly soft. "This will act as your bonds."

He replaced the silk with a handful of lace. "It's a deep burgundy. Touch it, pet." Brie played with the lace in her hands, noting the roughness of it. "This will be caressing your body in a few minutes."

The last thing he placed in her hand was something leather. She could smell it even before he handed it to her. She felt it with her fingers, instantly identifying it as a glove. She wondered at its significance.

Marquis Gray took it from her and left her side again. When he returned, she heard him chuckling under his breath. Brie held out her hand, but he lifted her other hand and placed the item in both. She was worried when she felt something heavy that also smelled of leather. She caressed it with her fingers and a cold chill gripped her heart. One end was a hard handle, and the other had numerous leather tendrils. *A flogger.*

He leaned in close to her ear, his warm breath on her neck. "I am an expert at what I do. By the time I finish, you will be begging me for more." She felt her loins contract in fear and excitement. She remembered how contented Lea had looked after spending time with

Marquis. Maybe it would be enjoyable for her, too.

"Are you ready, pearl?"

"Yes, Marquis Gray."

"No… I think for today's session I would prefer that you call me Master."

She remembered when she'd slipped up and called him Master in class. It had been embarrassing then, but now the name held power. She was almost afraid to call him by it. "Yes…" She paused, then added, "Master."

"Good." He took the flogger, and she heard him move the small chest beside her. She heard the thuds as he dropped the items back into it. "Put your hands behind your head."

Brie crossed her hands behind her neck and he quickly bound her wrists together. She felt the ends of the long, silk ribbon tease the small of her back. Then she heard him slide something across the floor. "Kneel." She slowly knelt down and felt the give of a mat beneath her. She held her back straight, her feet tucked under her ass.

"Do you realize how beautiful you are right now?" he murmured. "Black lace covering your eyes, the black silk cascading down your back from your wrists and those delectable nipples hard with anticipation for what is yet to come…"

He leaned in even closer and said, in a barely audible whisper, "Clark and Coen wanted to dismiss you after they learned of Thane's breach of protocol last night." Marquis Gray had given her a gift by confirming Sir's first name, but the joy of that was tempered by the knowledge that all of the trainers knew the nature of her intimate encounter with Sir. He continued, "But Gallant and I don't believe such obvious talent should suffer for Thane's little indiscretion." He moved to her other ear. "Prove those two wrong, my little pearl. Show them that you are more than Thane's plaything."

He stood up and said in a commanding voice, for everyone to hear, "Lean forward more."

Brie did as she was told and held her breath while she waited for the sting of the flogger. Instead, Marquis Gray's touch was light as he rubbed the lace against her skin. The roughness of it felt like a gentle scratch, and Brie relaxed. He rubbed her upper back just under the shoulder blades on both sides of her spine. When there was a pleasant warmness to the area, he began gently slapping her skin with the flat of his palm. It reminded her of a doctor tapping the vein just before the poke of a needle.

She sighed nervously. Her body was starting to tingle in anticipation of her first real flogging, but this wasn't punishment. It was somehow sensual—a completely different animal.

She heard him rifle through the chest. "We are warming up, pearl. To make this a pleasurable experience, I need to get your endorphins flowing." With that, she heard and felt the stinging slap of the leather glove. She gasped out of surprise, although it didn't exactly hurt. "What is your color?" he asked.

Brie realized he was asking how she was doing and answered immediately, "Green."

"Fine." He brushed her hair to the side so he had free access to her back. His touch suddenly had a different feel. Her body was attuned to it, hungry for it.

He addressed the other girls when he spoke. "Never let an amateur practice flogging on you. It can be a harmful activity if a novice attempts it. Understand that there are only certain areas on the human body that can be flogged without causing damage. Choose an experienced Dom or have your Dominant study and practice on inanimate objects before he or she ever lays a hand on you. Am I making myself perfectly clear?"

The girls must have nodded because Marquis Gray turned his attention back to Brie, tracing a circle on her back before slapping the area with the glove. The tingling in her body increased as he continued to strike her with the glove with a constant, rhythmic pattern. It gave her body the chance to anticipate each hit, making the little electrical shockwaves of each contact more enjoyable.

"Color, pearl?" he said in a low, lustful tone.

"Green."

"Are you ready for more?"

Her heart quickened. "Yes, Master."

His baritone laugh caused her juices to flow. "Ah, I like hearing that word come out of your mouth." She heard him discard the glove and assumed he was picking up the flogger. In her mind, it was a jet black one with fifty tails. She could just imagine how she looked, her hands still at her neck bound by the black silk, her eyes covered in lace, her chest panting rapidly, the skin on her back red from the leather. Then there was Marquis Gray, poised behind her, ready to lash her with the menacing-looking flogger. What were the other girls thinking? How did it make Sir feel?

Brie cleared her mind and readied herself for the first hit. She had *thought* she was ready, but she was not. The multiple tails hit the right side of her back with a loud thud, and she yelped.

"Color?" he asked.

"Yellow."

"Perfect." Her Dom stroked her hair with his free hand, causing a river of tender sensations. "Your endorphins are starting to flow now. Do you feel it?"

She nodded, hoping he would continue stroking her hair, but he pulled back and announced, "I am going to flog you on the other side now. Give in to the sensation. Embrace it." She heard the movement in the air before she felt the impact. A loud thud echoed in her head. This time, she whimpered softly. Although his swing had been a little harder, it left her feeling warm.

"Color?"

"Yellowish green."

He chuckled. "I think you are properly warmed up, pearl."

He moved away from her and then the sound of Mozart suddenly filled the auditorium. He placed something in front of her and said, "Lean against it. You'll need the support when you enter subspace." She leaned her chest against what must have been a stool.

He stood behind her and said soothingly, "Enjoy the ride."

She took a deep breath, feeling almost lightheaded. There was no fear, only excitement for what was about to happen. The rain of blows began in steady rhythm with the music. Each thud of contact sent waves of electricity through her body. The sensation started at the point of contact, but grew as it flowed through her. It reminded her of a drop of rain landing in still water. Tears of pleasure squeezed themselves through the blindfold as she let the music and sensations carry her.

Brie was disappointed when he stopped. He lightly brushed the curve of her neck with his fingers. She moaned softly at the intimate contact. Then he took the silk hanging from her wrists and teased her skin with the ends of it. She purred as the cool silk trailed over her warm back. Her whole body focused on the erotic feel of it.

"Color?" he growled lustfully. It was obvious from the tone of his voice that he found his role sexually exciting.

"Green, Master. Oh, so very green."

"More then?"

"Please…"

She readjusted herself against the stool, biting her lower lip as she waited. The music had changed to a slower melody, and Marquis Gray adjusted his lashes accordingly. They were coming harder now, bringing with them jolts of electrical sensation. A tingling started in her toes, then slowly rose through her body until it seemed to burst from her head. She moaned in spiritual ecstasy. It was intense, like an orgasm.

She was barely aware when he stopped and tried talking to her. Brie had to concentrate to make out his words. "Nod if you are still green."

With great effort, she nodded slightly.

"Good, pearl. I think that is enough for your first

time."

Brie slowly shook her head.

"You are going to have to trust me that you've had enough."

"Please, Master," she managed to whisper.

He chuckled lustfully. "Begging for it, are we?"

A Cuddle & Dismissal

S he heard him throw the flogger in the chest, and then he gently untied her wrists. She put them down, but her arms felt like foreign objects. Marquis Gray picked her up in his thin but deceptively strong arms and carried her from the stage. Instead of returning Brie to her seat, he carried her to the back of the auditorium, where she heard an assistant open a door.

He put her down on a soft bed and then lay beside her, pulling her close to him. She could feel the rigidness of his cock through his thick jeans as it rested against her buttocks. Marquis untied the blindfold, and she saw they were in a small room lit by soft candlelight. He used the lace of her blindfold to caress her skin, starting with her shoulder, moving over her breasts, lingering near her bellybutton. She lay there with her eyes closed in total bliss, focusing on the delicious sensation.

He nuzzled her neck as he let go of the lace and trailed his fingers to her bare mound. "Your pussy is gorgeous. Spread it open for me." She did so without thinking.

His fingers swirled over her clit and she pressed against him, moaning softly. She felt his cock twitch in response. It didn't take much before she was squirming against his hand, ready to come.

"Would you do another session of your own free will, pearl?"

"Of course," she answered dreamily.

"What's my name?"

"Master."

He flicked her clit rapidly until she tensed. Her wet pussy pulsed rhythmically against his hand as her orgasm crashed over her. The pleasant feeling of the climax lingered long after it was over. She expected him to take her, but he didn't move. She turned her head and whispered, "I would like to please you."

Marquis frowned. "Copulating outside of the stage is not allowed for a trainer. That's where Thane made his mistake."

"But he runs the school. Can't he bend his own rules?"

"Not if he wants this school to maintain its reputation."

Brie turned to face him and gazed longingly into his dark eyes. "I won't tell. I want to please you."

He turned her back around and pressed up against her. "No. Not tonight."

Brie started to shiver uncontrollably. Marquis Gray wrapped his arms tighter around her. "Why I am so cold?" she asked, snuggling closer to him.

"You're coming down from the high. It's a natural part of the experience." He nuzzled her neck again. Brie felt completely safe in his arms. She would never have suspected the frightening ghost-man had such a soft side to him.

The door opened and Sir entered the room. Brie looked up at him dreamily and smiled, forgetting that she was naked, all cuddled up in Marquis Gray's arms. He averted his eyes and spoke to Marquis. "The panel is ready to explain tomorrow's auction to the group."

"She still has another fifteen minutes or so. Don't worry. I'll explain it to her."

Sir nodded and left the room, slowly closing the door behind him. If she hadn't been so relaxed, Brie might have worried about the expression on his face. But the way she was feeling, nothing could touch her bliss. "What about the auction?"

"Tomorrow the three of you will meet in the commons, where a short auction will be held. The Doms in attendance have been apprised of your fantasy and the Dom with the winning bid will act it out with you."

"What fantasy?"

"The one you wrote in your journal today."

Brie shook her head. "What? I thought that was private."

He growled in her ear, "What better way to introduce you to the submissive lifestyle than to have your most cherished fantasy lived out in real life?"

Delightful tremors coursed through her. "I never thought of experiencing it in real life."

"You are in for quite an experience. The Dom who wins the bid will take you to his place of residence and play with you throughout the day. Afterwards, he will return you to the school for a short debriefing."

She turned to him again. "I'm going to leave the school?"

"Of course. We want you to have a real-life experience. Every Saturday you will spend time with a different Dom, living out your fantasies or his."

Brie shivered again at the chill attacking her body. She nestled into Marquis' embrace, needing his warmth. "Is there anything special I should do?"

"Remember what you have been taught. The Doms understand that you have had only three days of training."

"It sounds like tomorrow will be an interesting day." She sighed gleefully.

"I promise it will be an eye-opener for you."

"Can trainers bid?" she asked, half joking.

"No, but I'm curious. Who would you choose?" he growled in her ear.

"You and Sir for a little DP."

He snorted. "Will never happen, I guarantee it."

"Why not?"

"Never mind why not." He moved away from her, gathering Brie's clothes from a chair and handing them to her. "Get dressed. You'll have a long day tomorrow."

She knew she had said something wrong, but was too content to question him further. She slipped on her hose and skirt, then asked Marquis for help when she couldn't get her corset tight enough. "Sting said I should wear it tighter."

He came over to her and helped her with the ties, almost taking her breath away when he pulled the cords.

"Yes," she squeaked, "that's good."

"Do you do everything we suggest?"

"Of course—that's why I'm here, isn't it?"

"A natural sub through and through." He tucked a curl behind her ear before opening the door to the auditorium.

Their private time was over and his countenance instantly changed. He returned to being distant and menacing. She walked away from him, feeling a little shell-shocked by the change in him after their tender moment together.

Brie could see that the other girls were getting set to leave. Lea looked in her direction and gave her a thumbs-up. She returned it with a little grin. Mary completely ignored her, standing up to leave with a self-satisfied look on her face.

"Miss Wilson and Ms. Taylor, remember to get here early. The auction starts promptly at three in the afternoon, and you will return here at eleven for an hour-long debriefing. Get plenty of sleep. You should be fully rested for tomorrow's event," Mr. Gallant encouraged.

Brie wondered what he was doing there. Were they planning to kick her out of the program tonight? The possibility frightened her.

Ms. Clark confirmed her worst fears when she stated, "Miss Bennett, you will stay after class."

Lea looked her way and put her hands together in a sign of prayer before she left. Mary smiled knowingly and sauntered out of the auditorium as if she owned the place.

Brie looked at the ground to appease Ms. Clark and

asked, "Where would you like me to sit?"

"You are expected to stand before the panel," the Dominatrix ordered.

She walked before them, her heart beating wildly. To find her calling and then have it snatched from her seemed incredibly unfair. She wasn't going to stand for it!

Brie looked up and stared each of them in the eye. "I have done nothing wrong. You have no reason to expel me from the Training Center." Brie looked down once she had finished speaking, but not before she noticed the look of disgust on Ms. Clark's face.

"You have been called here tonight because of Mr. Davis' indiscretion. In the twenty-five years this school has been running, we have never had such a breach of decorum," Mr. Gallant informed her. "Such an act threatens the integrity of the program."

"It was my mistake," Sir asserted. "Miss Bennett should not be made to pay."

Master Coen sounded displeased and snapped, "Maybe you should resign as headmaster."

"If you feel it is necessary."

Ms. Clark interjected, "We cannot afford to lose Mr. Davis. The school has been extremely successful under his leadership. I say the sub must go!"

"Miss Bennett shows promise," Marquis Gray said with conviction. "It would be irresponsible for this school to allow her talent to be wasted because of a trainer's misstep."

Master Coen countered, "I have reason to suspect you have also fallen under the spell of this student. I believe she is a detriment to the school, not an asset."

"How can grown men talk about this woman as if she has mystical powers?" Mr. Gallant asked. "Miss Bennett is a hardworking, dedicated student who has done nothing but attempt to meet our rigorous stand-ards. If we have trainers who lack restraint, that does not reflect badly on her. Miss Bennett is *not* the one to blame in this situation."

"Which brings me back to my original suggestion," Master Coen stated. "I believe Thane should step down as headmaster."

There were several grunts on the panel. Brie could stay silent no longer. "Do I have permission to speak?"

Several of the Doms answered at the same time. Most were yes, but one or two voices said no. Sir answered for them all. "Yes, Miss Bennett."

She looked him in the eye, willing herself not to cry. "I refuse to be the reason you resign from this school. As much as I want my training to continue, it is not worth that." She held her head up and announced to the panel, "I willingly quit the program." She turned away from them and started towards the door.

You can cry later, she reminded herself. She heard furi-ous whispering behind her. Before she made it to the door, Master Coen called out, "Return before the panel, Miss Bennett."

She held her breath as she walked back to them.

The auditorium was deathly silent. Brie felt the eyes of all five on her. She wasn't sure if it was a power play on their part, but she stood quietly, looking at the floor the way a proper submissive should.

Sir finally spoke. "The panel has decided to reject your request to leave the program. You will continue on as a student here and I will continue as headmaster."

Ms. Clark added angrily, "You are expected to follow our commands to the letter. Do you understand, Miss Bennett? When I say jump, you'd better jump."

Brie did not look up, but answered clearly, "Yes, Mistress Clark."

"Additionally," Marquis Gray said, "you shall not fraternize with any of the trainers outside the confines of your training."

Again, Brie kept her head down and nodded. Yes, they were allowing her to stay in the program, but they were still acting as if she was the problem. Well, she would prove them wrong.

"I understand, Master Gray." She wondered if he was smiling or frowning at her choice of title.

"Brie," Mr. Gallant said, "I want you to look at me."

She held her head up and gazed into his caring eyes.

"We are here to provide you with the best training possible. I encourage you to go forward as if this had never happened. You are correct. You have done nothing wrong and you will not be punished for it. Your only job is to learn. We will take care of the rest."

"Thank you, Mr. Gallant."

"You are dismissed."

She bowed to the panel and left. Her heels clicked loudly, echoing in the auditorium. Instead of it being a lonely sound, she imagined that her footsteps resonated with power.

To Sir, with Love

What a crazy night!

Brie had gone from the joy of having spent time with Sir alone, the evening before, to the torture of a Brazilian, of being forced to watch Sir as he mounted Mary, and of almost being kicked out of the program. It had been more than a normal girl could take. But…fully realizing her own power as a submissive and following that up with an intense experience with Marquis Gray had given Brie a high like none she'd experienced. There was nothing else on earth that could have made her feel this good!

She lay on her bed, looking up at the ceiling. Despite that incredible feeling, something was needling her heart. She glanced over at her video equipment. This would be the first weekend that she wouldn't be filming a short. It seemed a little tragic. Even though she hadn't found success as a filmmaker yet, she still dreamed she would, someday. Was it possible becoming a submissive would steal that from her?

No freakin' way!

She got off the bed and set up her camera. Maybe she wouldn't have time to make creative shorts, but she could certainly record her thoughts as she went through her submissive training. Maybe she could make it into a documentary and sell it afterwards.

Brie reapplied her makeup and fixed her hair before sitting down in front of the camera. She spent the next forty-five minutes going over her thoughts and impressions of the first two days—minus her tryst with Sir—and titled the sitting *The Weeding Out Period*. It was amazing to realize that over those two short days she'd discovered so much about herself. Brie had enjoyed sexual encounters with men she would have never considered partnering with before. She'd also addressed a deep-seated anxiety that had controlled her life since childhood, based on abuses she had suffered. Her dark Dom, Baron, had helped to soften her fear of African American men, and she sincerely hoped she would have further sessions with him.

As far as the submissive lifestyle went, she'd learned simple etiquette and experienced personal and very real disappointment when she, as a sub, had failed to obey her Dom. What she hadn't understood until now was that pleasing another, giving her power over to him, was a heady experience. It was a turn-on like no other. She was *hooked*.

She signed off for the night, too tired to record her thoughts about Day Three's lessons. It was probably for the best. It was still too fresh for her. She needed time to go over the many levels of pain and pleasure she'd experienced in that short duration of time.

Brie closed her eyes and snuggled into her blanket. She was surprised that the needling was still pricking her heart. Then it hit her—the look in Sir's eyes when he'd seen her with Marquis Gray.

She was wide awake now. The look in his eyes had been as vulnerable as it had been after their intimate session together. It hadn't been a look of hurt. No, it had been something much deeper than that. He'd knowingly risked his career just to spend time alone with her when he could easily have taken her virginity on the stage. Why would he have done that?

Brie knew the answer: he'd wanted it to be private. They hadn't had to share that moment with anyone else. Her heart began beating rapidly as she began to understand just how much he cared for her. His claim about the protection collar meaning nothing was a bunch of bull. They both wanted to claim each other, but her current training prevented it for another five weeks. Could she survive for that long? *Yes!*

In fact, Brie was more determined than ever. At the end of the training, she would be the perfect sub. Sir had been willing to give up his position so that she could continue. She would make the most of her training and prove to everyone that she deserved to stay. By the end of it, she would force Ms. Clark and Master Coen to eat crow.

She looked over at the empty pillow on the left side of her bed. She imagined Sir laying his head on it, looking at her solemnly. Brie got up and retrieved her little bullet 'toy'—her best friend, at a time like this.

She turned it on full blast, knowing no other speed

would do, and then placed the frantically vibrating toy against her clit. *Yum...* Her body instantly relaxed and she gave in to the delicious vibration.

Brie closed her eyes, imagining Sir's naked body next to hers. He looked distressed, so she lightly caressed the crease of his brow. "I think sometimes a good Dominant needs the chance to let go," she told him. He smiled slightly but said nothing.

She took matters into her own hands and straddled his hips, rubbing her groin against his hardening cock. "You don't have to say or do anything. Just lie there and let your sub love on your body." She whipped off her top and smiled down at him.

His eyes softened as he reached up and caressed her breasts. Brie tugged and pulled on her nipples, envisioning that her hands were his. She leaned over so he could take her nipple in his mouth.

Sir sucked hard, the way he had the other night. She moaned as her body responded to the memory of it. "Sir, I like that you know what my body needs."

After giving ample attention to one, he switched to the other nipple. She cried out again, loving the way he suckled her. This time she felt a small contraction in her loins. Her fantasy was definitely working.

She left him for a moment to pull off her panties and skirt. She wanted him to admire her bare little pussy. She stood up on the bed and straddled him so he could get a nice, long look. "Do you like?" she asked playfully. He nodded and reached up to touch it.

Brie brought her finger to her pussy and played with it, just as Sir was in her mind. Her body wiggled and squirmed at the intimate contact. "You're so wet, Brie," he said hoarsely.

"Wet for you, Sir." She slowly descended on his rigid manhood. Even though she was wet and ready for him, his cock still stretched her. She groaned in delight.

"Are you going to fuck me, sub?"

"Yes, Sir. This sub is going to fuck you to her heart's content."

He chuckled beneath her. Oh, how Brie loved the sound of his laughter! She pushed his entire length into her moist tunnel and then began rocking against his shaft. He grabbed her buttocks with his large hands, pushing himself in deeper.

Brie pushed the toy inside her opening and felt it vibrate against her vaginal walls. She imagined his cock exploring her depths and thrust her hips to meet his mighty thrusts. In her mind, she pressed her hands against his chest so she had the leverage to grind harder.

"You want it deep, don't you?" he growled.

"As fast and deep as I can take it, Sir." Brie returned the bullet to her sensitive clit. It twitched pleasantly. *Getting close…*

She pulled herself up to the tip of his cock and then slid back down on it. He liked it so much that he lifted her to do it again. "God, there is nothing as beautiful as that," he groaned, and then he threw his head back. "I'm going to come if you don't stop."

"Ah, but that's my decision, isn't it? I'm in control here."

He gazed at her lustfully. As a talented Dom, he had to control his orgasms for scenes, but not this time. She leaned over to his ear and whispered, "I want you to give in to the pleasure completely. Let yourself come with no thought for anyone else."

He grunted in frustration. "I can't."

She pulled herself up again and slowly, ever so slowly, descended back onto his glistening shaft. "I *need* to feel you come inside me, Sir."

He could only watch her for so long and then he growled, grabbing her waist as he pumped her up and down on his hard cock. She felt tears come to her eyes as he let himself go, using her body solely for his pleasure. Those three little words were on the tip of her tongue, but even in her fantasy, she could not say them.

Instead, she let the first wave of her orgasm take over. Her hip muscles tensed as a tremendous burst of sexual energy coursed through her, making her nipples hard. Her screams echoed through her bedroom, but she didn't care. If Mr. Nguyen on the top floor could hear it and was getting his jollies from her passionate cries, so be it.

Brie lay there trembling afterwards, her whole body tingling from the intensity of the orgasm. She turned off her toy and looked up at the ceiling again. As she fingered the little black collar around her neck, she murmured, "Sir, I hope somehow you felt that. It was amazing!"

She snuggled back in her blanket, her body now satiated enough to rest. A half-smile played about her lips as her eyelids grew heavy. There was no doubt that tomorrow was going to be an adventure. Even so, nothing could compare to a session with Sir. *Nothing.*

Before her Auction

B rie did not wake up until eleven the next morning. After such a challenging day at the Submissive Training Center, it seemed her body had needed time to recover. She shivered in delight at the thought that a Dom was going to win her in an auction in the afternoon, then take her to his place to reenact her most cherished fantasy.

Her Indian warrior fantasy was one she had cherished and orgasmed to for years. She wasn't sure how the Dom would be able to pull it off, but she was anxious to find out!

She rolled out of bed and walked before the mirror to examine her Brazilian wax job. Her pussy looked completely different hairless. She could clearly see the outline of her clit in the reflection of the mirror. It surprised her how sexy it looked. She turned around and bent over. Her small rosebud of an asshole looked all pink and inviting. Her bare pussy lips beckoned to be taken. *Yep, it's a nice look*. Despite the pain of yesterday, she decided it had definitely been worth it.

Brie took a nice, long bubble bath. She needed the calming effect hot water gave her. Today, she would have to prove herself to Ms. Clark and Master Coen, both of whom wanted her out of the program. She thought it unfair that they blamed her for the tryst she'd had with Sir after school hours. Really, it had been Sir's fault, but she wasn't about to complain. Having him take her anal virginity in the privacy of the bondage room had been pure ecstasy. He had almost been asked to resign because of it, and the revelation of that still shook her to the core.

Sir had been the one who'd invited her to join the Submissive Training Center in the first place. She remembered, with a giggle and a snort, the recording she'd made of herself playing with a miniature phallus and crying out Sir's name.

She fingered the thin collar around her neck. He'd given the protection collar to her in order to prevent other Doms from claiming her before the end of the course, but it was clear (at least to her) that by giving her the collar, Sir had really meant to keep her for himself. She would still experience the sexual pleasures of other Doms during her training, but the collar meant they weren't allowed to fraternize with her outside the confines of the school. In the same vein, she would have to watch Sir train and enjoy the pleasure of the other subs. Would she be able to handle that for the next five-and-a-half weeks? She wasn't sure.

One thing Brie was sure of was that she would grad-uate from the program as the best damn sub they'd ever had. She was determined to learn *everything* the school had to offer. She would practice until she became skilled and make the trainers who wanted her out of the program admit their mistake. That would be her crowning glory—the day Ms. Clark and Master Coen asked for her forgiveness for doubting her exceptional abilities. Oh, what Brie wouldn't give to smack Ms. Clark on the ass for that!

Brie rubbed her skin with special oils that left a fresh, but not overpowering, floral scent. She wanted today's Dom to savor the smell of her when he buried his head in her neck or between her thighs…

She shivered again. Would these Doms be from the school, or would they be complete strangers from the local area? The not knowing and not having control over who would win her had a dangerous element she found enthralling.

She got to the Training Center before two-thirty. They had been instructed to come a half-hour early to receive last-minute instructions. The four regular trainers were already there. It took everything in Brie not to look up and gaze at Sir's face. She felt a warm contraction in her nether regions when she thought about her fantasy of the night before. Had he fantasized about her as well?

Ms. Clark spoke first. "You will stand behind the partition until your name is called. You are to walk onto the stage and face the audience, but with your eyes cast downward." She said the last part harshly. Brie knew the comment was directed at her. "After the winning bid is made, you will wait for your Dom to escort you off the stage. Remain by his or her side until all three of you have been auctioned off. At that point, you will follow your Dom out of the Center."

Master Coen continued, "Remember that you represent our school now. How you behave outside the school is just as important as inside these walls. We will be asking your winning Doms to critique you."

Sir's warm, velvety voice caressed Brie's ears. "I need your eyes on me."

She looked up and breathed in deeply, basking in his natural authority. He glanced briefly at her and then looked at the other two girls. "Yesterday you provided us with a fantasy. Your Doms will be acting that out with you today, but I want you to read through it before the bidding starts. It is imperative there is nothing in there you would not want played out. Sometimes what we enjoy in our minds does not make for enjoyment in real life."

He handed each of them their fantasy journals back. Brie made sure to lightly brush against his hand when she took hers from him. The simple contact set her heart aflutter, but he did not react.

"Read over what you have written. If there is anything that might cause problems, let me know now and we will pass it on to your Dom. This is meant to be a stimulating learning experience, not a challenge."

Brie opened her journal and read her entry. She smiled and blushed as she perused the story. Nope, there wasn't a single thing she would change. She was extremely curious about how her Dom was going to pull it off.

She shut her book and stood looking forward, taking in Sir's charming looks using her peripheral vision—that strong jaw, those kissable lips and his trim, muscular body. *So, so fine…*

"Is there anything you wish to eliminate from your fantasies?" he asked.

Lea shook her head and giggled, "Nope, it looks good to me, Sir."

"I agree," Mary, a.k.a. Blonde Nemesis, answered.

Sir glanced at Brie last. *Breathe*, she commanded herself. "I am pleased with my fantasy, Sir."

He nodded in response, and she swore she could see a twinkle in his eye. "Look through it one more time. There might be small details you have overlooked that may cause undue stress. This is important. Don't take this lightly."

Brie perused it again: Indian warrior on a horse, the chase, virginal captive, a fearsome rival warrior, the taking of her innocence. Yep, it all sounded yummy. The other two glanced through their journals as well and all three shook their heads. Marquis Gray collected the journals from them and handed the stack over to an assistant. "Now that issue has been addressed, I want to remind you that you will return here tonight for a debriefing after your encounter. It is imperative to go over your experiences while they are still fresh. We will discuss what worked, what didn't work and how you could have improved the scene for both you and your Dom. Keep those questions in the forefront of your mind as you go through the day. You want to make the most of this experience. It is not just about your personal enjoyment."

Brie nodded slowly, thankful for the reminder. Everything was a learning experience; she should never forget that.

Sir added, "You have ten minutes before the auction. Feel free to partake of the refreshments while you wait. We will see you out on the stage."

After the four trainers had left, Lea grabbed Brie and jumped up and down, singing, "I'm so excited, I just can't hide it!"

Brie laughed, partly in response to Lea's attempt at singing the ancient eighties song and partly because of her own nervousness. "What's your fantasy, girl?"

She grinned. "I've always had this sexy fantasy of a doctor taking advantage of innocent ol' me! 'Here, Ms. Taylor, let me examine your breasts...' Oh-em-gee! I'm getting wet just thinking about it."

"I guess I can see how that could get a girl hot."

"What about you, Brie?"

She looked down at her feet shyly. "Oh, I have this thing for dangerous Indian warriors."

"Nice! And you, Mary?" Lea asked.

Blonde Nemesis looked at them both and growled, "Like I would tell you."

"Stick in the mud!" Lea complained.

Mary ignored her and spoke to Brie. "I don't get why you're still here. I thought they kicked you out last night."

"Sorry, Mary. I'm never leaving this place, so you might as well get used to it and stop acting like such a bitch."

Mary's eyes narrowed, but she said nothing. Instead, she briskly moved to the other side of the room and ignored them.

Brie looked at all the delicate finger foods, but she couldn't eat. Her stomach was tied in knots—but in a good way. She grabbed a water bottle and downed as much as she could.

Ms. Clark came back and announced, "Ms. Taylor, you will be first. Miss Bennett will follow and Miss Wilson will end the auction. Do not speak while you wait your turn."

Brie obediently followed behind Lea, anxious and excited for the auction to begin.

The Winning Bid

Lea walked gracefully onto the stage. Brie could hear the low murmurs of several men. An announcer spoke to the small crowd. "Ms. Taylor is twenty-four and is a certified massage therapist outside these walls. Her trainers describe her as an enthusiastic submissive. Her fantasy involves the reluctant patient/doctor scenario. There are no additional changes to the sexual fantasy. I will start the bidding at one hundred."

The auctioneer started rapidly rattling off numbers as the bids steadily climbed to four hundred. "Going once... Going twice... Sold to Master Harris for four hundred dollars." Brie heard the footsteps as Master Harris collected Lea.

Brie's whole body went numb. She was next, but she was rooted to her spot.

"Next, we have Miss Bennett."

She tried to move, but her muscles wouldn't cooperate. Mary gave her a hard push and she fell forward, barely catching herself before she walked out onto the stage. She paused and gathered herself, keeping her back straight, her lips supple and her body in a pleasing pose.

"Miss Bennett is twenty-two, with a bachelor's degree in filmmaking outside these walls. Her trainers describe her as difficult, but teachable."

Brie felt her heart drop. *Difficult…? Really? Damn you, Ms. Clark!* A young male voice spoke softly in a guttural language, which was followed by a low, rumbling chuckle.

"Her fantasy involves the Indian warrior claiming his virginal captive. There are no additional changes to her sexual fantasy…"

Brie heard someone in front of her clear his throat in an attempt to get her attention. She snuck a glance and saw Tono standing there. She looked back down, trying hard not to smile.

Ms. Clark barked, "Stop the auction!" Her stilettos clicked up to the stage as she rushed over to Brie. "You *still* defy me."

Tono spoke from the crowd. "Do not punish her. I was seeking her attention."

"You know as well as I do that a submissive is responsible for following orders. She was told to keep her eyes down. I don't care if the whole lot of you were calling out her name. Miss Bennett's eyes should have stayed glued to the floor." To Brie, she hissed, "I will not tolerate this act of disobedience." She asked the three other trainers, "Do any of you have a blindfold?"

"I do," Marquis Gray answered, amusement coloring his voice. He walked onto the stage and handed a strip of lace to her.

Ms. Clark tied the blindfold overly tight. What she

didn't suspect was that instead of humiliating Brie, it gave her power. Now that Brie didn't have to worry about keeping her eyes down, it was actually freeing. When Ms. Clark walked away, she held her head up a little higher, but still at a respectful angle.

The auctioneer stated, "As I said before, there are no changes to her fantasy. I will start the bidding at one hundred."

"Four hundred," Tono said, his voice loud and clear. Brie squealed silently, excited at the prospect of spending a whole day alone with him.

She heard the low rumblings of the guttural language and then the young man's voice rang through the room. "Five hundred."

Brie felt the hairs go up on the back of her neck.

Tono confidently answered, "Six hundred."

The auctioneer asked for seven hundred. When no one spoke, he rattled off, "Going once... Going..."

The foreigner spoke and the young man called out, "Seven hundred."

Tono immediately followed with a bid for eight hundred. Brie's heart beat rapidly as she waited. She *only* wanted Tono as her Dom today. She crossed her fingers behind her back.

After a string of more foreign words, the young man blurted, "One thousand."

Brie heard Tono's low groan and her heart sank.

"The bid stands at one thousand dollars. Do I hear any other offers? Going once... Going twice... Sold to Rytsar Durov."

A chill coursed through her body. Tono wasn't going

to be her Dom? For a split second she was tempted to rip off the blindfold and run. However, her submissive spirit kicked in. *Take this opportunity to learn.*

She waited as his heavy footsteps ascended the stairs. A large hand grasped her arm and led her from the stage. His unfamiliar musk was clean, but rustic. He moved his hand from her shoulder onto the back of her neck. It sent a shiver down her spine that she was sure he could feel.

She heard Mary's named called next. "Miss Wilson is twenty-five and works as a pharmacist outside the confines of these walls." Brie had never suspected Nemesis was older than she was because the girl acted like such a brat. "Her trainers describe her as tenacious. Her fantasy consists of the spy interrogation and *infiltration*." There were a few chuckles throughout the room. "There are no additional changes to her sexual fantasy. I will start the bidding at one hundred."

The auctioneer rattled on until the bid was at four hundred. Brie felt sick when she heard Tono top the bid at five hundred.

Silence followed before she heard, "Going once... Going twice... Sold to Tono Nosaka for five hundred."

Why would Tono want my nemesis?

"This concludes today's auction. A simple reminder for the winners—once you have purchased a sub you are not allowed to bid on her again for the remainder of the training."

Her new Dom spoke to her in a deep baritone that reverberated through her body. The guttural way he spoke sounded Russian to her. The young man by his

159

side interpreted, "Rytsar Durov says you are under his rules now."

The Dom untied the blindfold and handed it over to an assistant. Brie bowed her head to let him know she was grateful. She suddenly liked this Dom who'd thwarted Ms. Clark in front of her face.

Rytsar lifted her head to get a better look at her, which gave her the opportunity to see who had purchased her. The man was tall and broad with a bald head, a strong jaw and riveting blue eyes. He was dressed in an expensive tailored suit and a power tie of blood red. She noticed an entourage of three attractive men behind him.

When he'd finished examining Brie, he smiled and looked over at the panel of trainers, mumbling something to his interpreter. The young man announced, "Rytsar believes that your definition of difficult is not the same as his."

They were the first to leave the Training Center. Rytsar guided Brie into an oversized black utility vehicle with his burly, unyielding arms. Once inside, he wrapped the seatbelt around her waist and slipped the buckle into place, double-checking to make sure it was secure. The rest of the men joined them in the spacious SUV.

Rytsar completely ignored her after that, speaking in Russian to the other men. Brie finally accepted that he wouldn't be asking anything of her during the trip, so she stared out of the window, wondering what he had in store for the next seven hours.

She couldn't help imagining Tono mounting Mary. It aggravated her to no end that he had bid for that horrible woman. Her thoughts were soon interrupted when they pulled up to a large glass house beside the ocean. The home was magnificent, with its modern architecture and pristine landscape.

Her large Russian Dom spoke to Brie matter-of-factly and then nodded to his interpreter. The young man addressed her after Rytsar had taken the time to unbuckle her. "Take off your shoes. Your safe word is *stoy*. Say it."

She repeated the word as she slipped off her six-inch heels, unsure why he was explaining that while they were still in the car.

He continued, "It means 'stop'. You will exit the vehicle now. I suggest you run. Rytsar has promised to cane you if you prove an easy catch."

She glanced over at Rytsar. His eyes held a wicked glint. She had no doubt he would follow through with the threat. As soon as he lunged for her, she threw open the door and bolted.

Brie ran for all she was worth, but looked back to check if he was really following. She screamed out in fear when she saw he was only a few paces behind.

Her flight instinct took over as she raced through the garden and headed towards the ocean. There was no thought process to her actions, simply the need to keep out of his reach. She attempted to dart to the side to throw him off, but he wasn't fooled and grabbed her arm. She cried out when his hand clamped down on her.

With the agility of a deer, she twisted out of his grasp and continued to run. The fear she felt was very real. She was deathly afraid of being caned, and just the act of being chased had her body humming in terror. There was no acting on her part; it was a rush of adrenaline spurred on by sheer panic.

She ran down the beach, but a rogue wave wrapped itself around her legs. She stumbled and nearly fell. She could hear his heavy breathing just behind her and shrieked. With a burst of speed that surprised even her, she escaped his clutches again.

Brie heard him chuckle softly. He changed tactics and edged her closer to the water. Even though she guessed his strategy, he was too fast for her to prevent it. The water hit her ankles again and this time she fell. He was on top of her in an instant. Brie screamed out in alarm, trying to fight him off.

He forced her to turn over and easily secured her arms above her head. His weight crushed her helpless body as another wave drenched them. His lips landed on hers, firm and commanding. When he broke the kiss, she gasped for breath, still struggling beneath his large frame.

Her Indian warrior had captured her...

Rytsar laughed as he pulled a leather tie from his pocket and bound her wrists together. Then he lifted her up, throwing her unceremoniously over his shoulder. He started towards the glass house, saying something she couldn't understand. His grip was tight—there was no escaping him. It gave her a thrill to know she was at his mercy now.

When he entered the house, she was bewildered to see it crowded with men. It looked like a party was in full swing with plenty of drinks, joking and manly laughter. The place quieted down as soon as Rytsar entered the home. He put her down and grabbed her chin with one of his massive hands. He forced her to look at him. His look was stern and dangerous but when he kissed her, there was a softness to his lips. She relaxed in his embrace, trusting her imposing Dom.

A stout man with spiky gray hair and a fearsome demeanor came up to them. He said something to Rytsar that must have been lewd, based on the tone he'd used and the dark look Rytsar was giving him. The vile man stroked Brie's arm as if he had a right to touch her. She recoiled and pressed against her Dom. Rytsar spoke harshly to the foul man, guiding her away, but the creep grabbed her arm and shouted at Rytsar in Russian.

Her Dom broke the loathsome man's unwanted grasp, moving her behind him as he participated in a heated exchange. The other men gathered around, enjoying the confrontation. The loathsome man tried to grab at her again, but Rytsar forcefully pushed him away. He picked Brie up and carried her through a set of doors on the other side of the room.

When he entered the bedroom, she noticed there was a support beam in the center of the massive space. He carried her past it and headed straight to the bathroom. After putting her down, he barked a single word, pointing to the toilet.

She blanched. Did he really want her to pee in front of him?

He barked the command again harshly, letting her know he wasn't amused by her lack of obedience. Swallowing hard, she awkwardly pulled her red thong down with her bound hands and sat meekly on the toilet. He nodded and exited, leaving the door wide open.

She glanced into the room while she washed herself clean and saw that he was changing out of his wet clothes. His chest was broad and his stomach rippled with muscles. She noticed a large tattoo in the shape of a dragon covering his left shoulder.

He returned wearing another suit. This time it was midnight black with an identical blood-red tie. He didn't look like an Indian warrior, but he certainly looked like a man of great power.

Rytsar picked her up and carried her to the support beam. He untied her wrists and bound them behind the pole before securing her feet. Next, he placed a gag over her mouth. She protested playfully with whimpers, which made him snort in amusement. He blindfolded her next and to make her sensory deprivation complete, he covered her ears with small headphones that blocked out all sound. Then he left.

She could feel the emptiness of the large room envelop her. At first, the total lack of stimuli was frightening but gradually she grew used to the all-encompassing silence. She stood there bound and alone, waiting for her warrior's return.

When she felt his presence again, she tensed. He took off the earphones and whispered in her ear. Although she could not understand his words, she believed he was listing all the things he planned to do to her. The commanding tone in his voice made her moist between her legs, and Brie moaned softly.

She was puzzled when he left her again. Outside the room, she could hear the men shouting and joking with one another. It was then that she realized this was his version of the village celebrating the raid in her fantasy. She appreciated his cleverness. To hear the men's revelry and to have the entire group know what was going to happen to her made it that much more exciting.

Her Dom came back and removed the gag next. He kissed her passionately, thrusting his tongue deep into her mouth, letting her know exactly how he was going to take her when the time came. He allowed her tongue to taste him and explore the ridges of his mouth before he pulled away and left her again.

His frequent visits, each accompanied by the removal of a restrictive item, made her hungry for his return. When Rytsar came the next time, he removed her blindfold. She looked into the blue eyes of her captor and quivered in delight. His stare was bursting with desire for her.

He pulled at the laces of her corset and let it fall to the ground. He leaned down and took her nipple into his mouth. She gasped when he sucked forcefully. His other hand played with her other nipple, pulling and tugging on it with equal vigor.

She threw her head back and groaned. Would he take her now? No—he left again. This time he did not return as quickly. She looked out of the large glass windows at the beach and watched the waves slowly rush in. It had a calming effect, giving her the patience to wait him out.

A lone jogger was heading down the beach. He seemed to look in her direction, but continued on. Soon, however, he was back and gawking into the bedroom at her half-naked body tied to the pole. Rytsar's entourage headed out and shooed him away.

Brie stood there for what seemed like hours, desperate for her warrior to come back for her. The waiting, she realized, was a seductive tactic. Being completely under his power, not having a say as to when or how he was going to take her, added a provocative element to the encounter. She needed him to return for her—she needed him *bad*.

Taking of an Innocent

Rytsar finally returned just as the sun was setting. She had to calm her breathing; her need for him was great. That changed when he shut the doors and approached her like a predatory animal. Instantly, her defenses were up and she whimpered in alarm.

He threw off his jacket, then removed his tie and shirt in fluid movements as he stalked around her, spewing nasty-sounding Russian words. His eyes glowed with unrestrained lust. She struggled in her bonds as he descended upon her. Brie was amazed that this Dom knew exactly how to play her emotions to elicit the desired response.

He grasped the back of her neck possessively, but this time he lingered centimeters from her lips before claiming them. She groaned in pleasure as his tongue violently ravaged her mouth. He was rough with her, but in a way that only made her hotter. She couldn't wait to be released from her bonds.

Rytsar slowly undid the ties, dragging out the action. When she felt the last of them fall, she tried to make a break for it. He grabbed her waist and wrestled her to the ground, crushing her small frame with his considerable weight.

Rytsar pulled her arms above her head and held her thin wrists with one hand while the other tugged at her thong. She struggled, but was defenseless to stop him. He threw it to the side and forced his fingers between her legs.

"No!" she cried, bucking her hips in an attempt to avoid the penetration, like a proper virgin captive. His chuckle was low when he felt her moist outer lips. He explored her smooth pussy, obviously enjoying the soft texture of her bare skin.

Unfortunately, there was no hiding how much she desired him, despite her feigned protests. His fingers inched inside, invading her moist, velvety depths. She stopped struggling, desperate for his attention after hours of waiting. Rytsar's talented manipulations had her body humming for release, but he denied her that by pulling his fingers out just as she was about to come.

Though he didn't lose his grip on her wrists, she heard him unzip his pants. Apparently, he was going to take her on the floor and not the luxurious bed a few feet away. It fit her fantasy. She moaned in delight when she felt his erection against her thigh. In her story, however, she was an innocent, so she wanted to give him a convincing battle.

Brie twisted out from under him, but couldn't move far due to the painful grip he had on her wrists. He easily positioned himself between her legs again, and this time there was no escape. She felt the round head of his cock penetrate her opening. He took his time, as if he were pushing into the tight opening of a virgin. She whimpered and cried, loving every second of his claiming. Once he had sunk his shaft fully inside her wet walls, he looked into her eyes and murmured what she assumed were Russian sweet nothings.

She stared up at him and took in his pure maleness. He was solid and imposing, with his sexy bald head, blue eyes and the naughty curve to his lips. He let go of her wrists, then lifted her hips up with both hands.

Brie threw her head back and moaned in unreserved pleasure. She was finally being fucked by her warrior. She arched her back and gave her body over to him.

His thrusts were strong and demanding. She had to remind herself to relax in order to take his entirety. She groaned as his speed and depth increased. He grabbed handfuls of her hair, grunting in his own pleasure while his tight pelvic muscles delivered repeated thrusts.

She could feel the burn on her back as they slowly inched across the carpet. It added to the brutish feel of their coupling. She wrapped her legs around his waist and cried out so the whole house could hear. "Rytsar, you're too big!" she screamed loudly, adding, "But I like it, oh, *yes*…! You make it hurt so good." Even though she knew he couldn't understand, she suspected some of his friends spoke English and it pleased her to promote his manliness to the crowd.

He grasped her face in his hands and kissed her deeply while he consumed her with his body. The ridge of his shaft rubbed that area deep inside that made her legs quiver uncontrollably. She purred into his mouth as he brought her to the edge, but then he stopped. Rytsar pulled out, chuckling wickedly under his breath.

He turned Brie onto her stomach and grunted out a command she assumed meant 'stay'. She lay on the carpet, breathless and needy. He came back to her less than a minute later and lay on top of her body with his rigid member between her butt cheeks. He lifted her pelvis up with one hand and pressed his lubricated cock against her asshole.

Brie hadn't been expecting him to take her anally, and she freaked. She clawed the floor, attempting to crawl away from him. He grabbed her and pulled her back. She screamed out in real fear then, tears running down her face.

Rytsar held her tightly in both arms and whispered soothingly, "Shhh…Shhh…" as his cock resumed its position and began pressing against her anus.

She froze and a small whimper escaped her lips. He wiped the tears from her cheeks, murmuring softly. A calmness took over when she realized he was going to be gentle. He continued to press his cock against her tight hole, demanding access. He was trying to claim a part of her she hadn't planned to give—just like the innocent in her fantasy.

Brie could call out the safe word and end this encounter, or she could give in and let her warrior have his way. A tingling sensation crept through her entire body as she made the conscious decision to surrender. She relaxed in his arms and stopped crying.

He lifted her ass higher to get a better angle and grunted as the head of his cock slipped into her resistant depths. He stayed still, letting her body get used to his manly girth.

Being taken this way gave her a greater sense of being possessed by the man. She panted softly, trying not to resist his masculine assault. When he started shallow strokes, she forced herself to breathe, helping her muscles to relax around his cock. He took his time, tender and kind, just as she'd always imagined her warrior would be—taking what he wanted, but doing it in a way that made her desire him more.

"Yes, my warrior. Take all of me," she moaned. He growled lustfully in her ear. Even though they did not speak the same language, they seemed to understand each other perfectly.

His thrusts became more pronounced as her body molded to him. He had already stimulated her inner spot when fucking her vaginally, and now he was caressing the same area at a different angle. She hadn't thought it was possible, but the first telltale signs of an orgasm were creeping up on her.

Her breath became more ragged the closer she got. Rytsar did not change his tempo. He continued the slow, steady pace, letting her climax build and increase. She turned her head towards him and he kissed her while he flexed his pelvic muscles with precision.

Rytsar was an accomplished lover who clearly knew a woman's body well. The muscles of her vagina contracted rhythmically when the orgasm hit. Her whole body tensed and she made little mewing noises as it overtook her. He pushed his cock in deeper, and then she felt it grow inside her before it started pulsating. He groaned as he came, kissing the nape of her neck.

The ending of their climaxes was interrupted by a knock on the door.

Rytsar barked something in Russian. The young man answered him earnestly, then he spoke in English. "Miss Bennett, the police are here. They wish to speak to you immediately."

Brie froze. What would the cops want with her? She hadn't done anything wrong!

Rytsar slowly disengaged, mumbling what sounded like Russian curse words. He barked towards the door as he held his hand out to Brie and helped her up.

The two went to the bathroom and thoroughly cleaned themselves. He seemed in no hurry to meet with the police. It made her wonder if he had something to hide, or whether this was a part of his scenario.

He wrapped her in a fluffy white bathrobe and then got re-dressed himself. He put his arm around her as he led her out of the bedroom. Two police officers stood at the front door. They looked visibly relieved when they saw Brie.

As she walked up to them, she noticed a third man. She had the distinct feeling she knew him when she looked into those crystal blue eyes. It threw her off and she subconsciously grabbed the collar around her neck.

The tallest of the officers spoke first. "Ma'am, we are sorry to disturb you, but this gentleman called to report a possible kidnapping and we needed to make sure you are all right."

She turned a deep shade of red. "I'm fine, officers."

Blue Eyes spoke. "When I saw you tied up I thought

you might be in trouble."

So he was the jogger on the beach! Brie stared at him more closely, certain his face was familiar to her. "I assure you that I am quite fine, although I appreciate the concern."

The other officer cleared his throat as he tipped his hat to her. "We apologize for the inconvenience. Obviously, we had to investigate, given the unique circumstances."

Rytsar barked something to his interpreter, who replied evenly, "If that is all, Rytsar Durov would like to return to his guests."

Blue Eyes looked around and seemed to note there were only men in attendance. He sputtered, "Are you sure everything is okay, Miss? We can take you from this place if you feel unsafe in any way."

She suddenly recognized who he was. He was the man who'd saved her from falling on the cement just outside the school. She played with her collar when she answered, "I am enjoying myself. There is no reason for you to be concerned, but thank you."

His gaze rested on the collar. After several seconds, it seemed to dawn on him what was going on and he looked at her apologetically.

The tallest officer nodded. "Have a good evening." To Rytsar, he added, "You should invest in curtains for that bedroom to avoid further misunderstandings."

Rytsar answered through the interpreter. "People should mind their own business instead of peeking into a man's bedroom." He slammed the door behind them.

My Joy

After the officers had left, laughter erupted through the house. Several men slapped Rytsar on the back. He did not take kindly to the attention and snarled at them. When the menacing Russian came up to Brie, Rytsar deftly maneuvered her out of his reach.

He spoke harshly to the uncouth man, who took one last hungry look at her before leaving the house. She sighed with relief, but then Rytsar picked her up and sat her on the large dining room table. He opened her robe and kissed her left nipple while fondling her other breast with his large hand. The other men gathered around.

Brie's heart started beating a mile a minute. Luckily, her experience on the stage during training had prepared her for an audience. He gently pushed her down onto the table and scooched her butt to the edge. His lips slowly traveled from her breasts, down her stomach to her bare snatch. He licked her moist folds with guttural satisfaction. She forgot the other men and closed her eyes, giving in to his expert tongue-lashing. She felt his fingers slip into her opening and caress her. Since she had last orgasmed so recently, it did not take much to start her legs quivering. She arched her back and moaned as he stroked her to a quick climax. All around her, Brie heard the appreciative grunts of the men as she thrust her pelvis into the air.

Rytsar kissed her clit reverently afterwards and then helped her off the table. He slid the robe off her shoulders and let it fall to the ground. She stood before him, naked except for Sir's collar. He barked something and the interpreter stated simply, "Please me."

She looked into the eyes of her warrior and smiled as she gracefully knelt down on the cold marble floor. She unbuckled his expensive leather belt and then unzipped his designer pants. They fell to the floor with a satisfying clang. He was not wearing underwear and his manhood was already impressively rigid.

Brie looked up at her Dom as she took his shaft with her lips. He grunted quietly when they made contact, but his expression remained stoic. She felt incredibly powerful on her knees, caressing her Dom's manhood with her mouth.

She heard the men around her shifting and making noises under their breaths. They wanted her—they *all* wanted her—but she was submissive only to one. She knew without question that Rytsar would not share her. His only intention was to show her off.

She took him deeper into her mouth while she stroked him with her hand. Brie twirled her tongue over his shaft and sucked and licked, her slurping sounds filling the silent room.

Through clenched teeth, he commanded something

more of her. She heard the interpreter say quietly, "Touch yourself."

Brie moved her fingers down to her pussy and opened her wet lips. She heard some of the men groan as she slipped two fingers inside. She sucked on Rytsar's shaft even harder, getting excited by her own stimulation. A deep groan resonated in his chest and she felt him grow between her lips.

She pulled her fingers back out and started flicking her clit furiously, moaning around his dick. He grabbed her head, forcing her to take his essence as he came. Brie surrendered to him, bringing both hands to his shaft as she swallowed his bitter warmth eagerly. To share this part of him was extremely satisfying.

She looked up at her Dom as she pulled away. Rytsar stroked her hair, growling softly, "*Radost moya.*"

The translator cleared his throat, obviously affected by the scene, and murmured, "My joy."

Brie smiled up at Rytsar. "My warrior."

The young interpreter translated her praise. Her Dom nodded and zipped up his pants before lifting Brie off the ground and crushing her to his chest. He barked a command to his entourage and then carried her back to the bedroom.

Rytsar laid her gently on the large bed. She gazed at her Russian Dom and purred. He was so masculine and clever, and had given her almost every aspect of her fantasy. He joined her on the bed and gathered her into his arms, pressing her head against his beefy chest while mumbling sexy Russian words. They rumbled from deep in his chest, reminding Brie of a kitten—okay, maybe a lion—purring. He'd been so wicked to show her off in front of his friends and then to leave them to salivate in the other room.

His interpreter knocked a short time later, saying something through the door. Rytsar grunted and got off the bed. He handed Brie her clothes, which had been cleaned and dried sometime during their interlude. He watched while she dressed, so she decided to put on a show for him. She made it as sexy as a striptease, only sensually covering up her body instead of exposing it. He grunted in appreciation.

Brie noticed a glint in his eye when he produced the leather binding and tied her wrists together. She wondered what else he had in mind as he escorted her out of the house, through the crowd of hungry men.

She gasped in surprise when she saw the glistening coat of a white stallion in the moonlight. Rytsar boosted her onto the impressive beast and deftly climbed up behind her. He dug into the animal's sides with his heels and it took off towards the beach. Brie leaned into Rytsar for balance, grinning from ear to ear. He slowed the horse to a walk near the water, letting the waves brush up against its hooves. The night was spectacular, with the moonlight reflecting off the water and the rushing sound of waves filling the cool air.

Brie could see a fire on the beach in the far distance. As they approached, she realized it had been started for them. She could see a blanket next to the fire pit. Rytsar jumped from his horse and pulled her off roughly. She squealed, completely defenseless due to her bonds.

He chuckled as he righted her and rubbed her arms

to warm her after the cold night's ride. He guided her closer to the fire and had her stand there while he tied the horse to a large piece of driftwood.

When he came towards her, his eyes reflected the fiery orange of the flames. It gave him a sinister look that she rather enjoyed. He pointed to the blanket and grunted a command. She wasn't sure what he wanted, so she knelt down on it. He shook his head and grabbed her waist, lifting her onto her hands and knees. It was difficult keeping her balance with her hands tied, but he didn't seem to care. She heard him unbuckling his belt. He was going to take her out in the open next to the fire.

His fingers disappeared under her little skirt and peeled off her panties, then he reached around and pulled down her corset just enough to expose her breasts to the frigid air. He rested his hard cock in between her butt cheeks, letting her know he was ready for her.

She arched her back gracefully and looked back at her Dom. His growl was low and lustful as he grabbed a fistful of her long brown curls and thrust his large cock into her pussy with one solid stroke.

Brie gasped at the sudden infiltration. He pulled her head back farther with one hand and guided his thrusts with the other. She cried out into the night as her warrior claimed his prize one more time. He fucked her hard and fast, with no thought to her pleasure. This was all about his need and his desires. She gave in to it, wanting to please him.

Apparently, the night air had given him special powers, because Rytsar was an animal. Skin slapped against skin as he repeatedly forced his cock deep inside her.

Brie did not suppress her vocalizations. She was loud and very expressive. "Yes, my warrior. Fuck your captive. Oh, God, I need this!" Brie grunted and moaned as he ravaged her pussy relentlessly.

The ocean added to the experience with its siren call. Feeling a part of nature, she looked up at the moon and gave a throaty howl when he finally came in her velvety depths. Rytsar collapsed next to her, murmuring, "*Radost moya.*"

Brie rolled over and smiled at him. With her wrists still tied, she ran her fingers over his full lips, looking into his deep blue eyes. "You are the perfect warrior," she told him, knowing he couldn't understand but hoping she was expressing it with her eyes.

He cupped her cheek in his large hand and kissed her. The two looked up at the few stars that could compete with the full moon. The horse nickered, patiently waiting for its master. Time seemed to have stopped for Brie—this was perfection. She felt a tear run down her cheek.

Rytsar wiped it away, and she smiled as she kissed each finger and then each of his cheeks before planting a sweet kiss on his lips. How else could she tell him that she was crying with sheer joy? He pressed her into his chest and they lay there in silence.

Eventually, he untied her hands and they both got up to dress. He helped her back onto the horse and they headed towards the glass house. Brie shed a few more tears as they approached his home. She didn't want their night together to end.

A Dangerous Secret

The stallion's hooves echoed off the pavement as they made their way up the driveway to the vehicle. Rytsar dismounted and caught her in his arms as she slid off the majestic beast. This time, he pulled her to him and kept his arm around her for the entire drive. Even though they were strangers, there was a feeling of incredible closeness after sharing such intimacy. She rested her head on his muscular chest, silently mourning the end of the evening.

The ride back to the school was far too quick. Rytsar helped her out of the car and guided her into the school with his hand resting on the back of her neck; it was a very possessive hold. Only his interpreter followed them inside.

They walked directly to the commons area where the auction had taken place. Instead of the stage, she saw a table with the four trainers, a table of refreshments and Lea, who was sitting on a chair facing the panel.

Lea smiled at Brie. It was obvious from the look on her face that she had had a spectacular time as well.

Rytsar Durov escorted Brie to the chair next to Lea's and then continued over to the trainers. Although they spoke in quiet tones, Brie picked up two words from the translator: 'pliable' and 'intriguing'. She smiled to herself. If she'd had to describe Rytsar, she would have said 'assertive', 'creative', and 'pure perfection'.

The smell of the food was getting to her. She hadn't eaten anything since noon and her stomach growled loudly in protest. *How unsexy is a rumbling stomach?* Luckily, no one seemed to have noticed.

Rytsar walked back over to her when he was finished. She stood up and looked obediently to the floor. He moved his lips to her ear. In perfect English, he whispered, "My joy."

Her eyes widened. *Was his interpreter just a ruse?*

He squeezed the back of her neck one last time and left.

Sir spoke, "Miss Bennett, feel free to partake of the food. We anticipated that you would need nourishment after your session." She looked up, chagrined and embarrassed that he had heard her stomach. However, when she met his stare she was struck by the burning desire in his eyes. She had to remind herself to breathe. Maybe he *had* shared that moment with her last night, when she'd pleased herself while she'd fantasized about him.

"Thank you, Sir." Brie walked to the table, her stomach suddenly full of butterflies. After that one glance, she could think of nothing but Sir.

"Do you realize who Rytsar Durov is, Miss Bennett?" Master Coen asked, after she'd sat back down with her plate. Brie shook her head demurely. "He is a prominent Dom in Russia. Rytsar just happened to be in the area this weekend. You had the potential of not only shaming yourself locally, but internationally as well."

Brie was eternally grateful she hadn't known who Rytsar was. It would have been way too much pressure to know he was a highly respected Dom. Just thinking about seeing him again made her stomach queasy, now that she was aware of his status.

Marquis Gray interjected, "As predicted, Miss Bennett proved her worth as a submissive."

"I was extremely uncomfortable with Durov's choice of a sub. Her willfulness makes her a wildcard." Ms. Clark shot Brie a disgusted look.

Sir spoke in her defense. "Rytsar had no complaints. I think you both underestimate Miss Bennett."

"I concur," said Marquis Gray.

Master Coen grumbled under his breath, "I would expect no less coming from you two."

"We were simply fortunate she didn't cause trouble," Ms. Clark stated, staring at her watch. She frowned and looked at Sir. "Where is Tono? He is never one to be late."

No sooner had she made that remark than an assistant entered the commons and handed Sir a message. He glanced at it and announced, "We have a problem." He handed the note down so each of the trainers could read it.

"I need to call Dr. Reinstrum. It is imperative we take care of this tonight, before more harm is done." Sir abruptly stood up and left the commons.

The trainers spoke quietly amongst themselves while the girls waited in frightened silence. Brie was no longer hungry and put her plate on the floor.

She observed Sir covertly when he returned.

He informed the panel, "The doctor will be here in fifteen minutes." Then he turned to Lea and Brie. "Ladies, there is no need for alarm. After we get all the particulars, I'll discuss what has happened with you. Until then, I ask for your patience and trust."

Everyone turned when the elevator doors opened and Tono came walking out, carrying Mary in his arms. He gently put her down in the seat beside Brie's and laid Mary's head on her lap. Blonde Nemesis lay there quietly, looking defenseless and vulnerable.

Brie lightly stroked her hair, shocked at the difference in the girl. *What could possibly have gone wrong?*

Tono turned to the trainers. "She did not disclose everything. There are demons in her past that resurfaced today."

Master Coen spoke up, "We are heartily sorry, Tono Nosaka. The girls were instructed not to keep any secrets. We apologize for her mistake."

"I have spent the last two hours helping her get to a place where we could return here."

Ms. Clark stated, "Obviously, we will return your bid."

Tono waved away her statement. "Just see that the girl gets the help she needs. I see real potential in her."

Sir replied, "I've already called Dr. Reinstrum to join us. Rest assured, Ren, we will do everything to help Miss Wilson recover from this experience."

Brie perked up. *So, Tono's first name is Ren?* It totally fit the man.

Sir got up and walked over to the girls. Just his mere presence had her heart fluttering, despite the dire circumstances. "Ren, do you mind joining me in my office so we can get specifics?"

"That would be fine." Tono gazed down at Mary with concern, then addressed Brie. "Take care of her, *toriko.*"

She was pleased that he'd called her by his pet name, but to avoid getting in trouble with Ms. Clark, Brie kept her eyes to the floor and only nodded in response. He left the room with Sir and a strained silence settled over the room. Brie continued to stroke Mary's hair, humming softly.

Ms. Clark growled, "That foolish girl has damaged the school's reputation."

Marquis Gray snarled at her, "We will discuss it later."

Brie looked down at Mary, worried she might be hurt by Ms. Clark's callousness, but the girl seemed oblivious to everything around her. "You're going to be all right, Mary," she whispered softly.

The instant Mary registered Brie's voice, she stirred in her lap. She looked around as if coming out of a trance and then immediately pulled away when she saw whose lap she was lying on.

"Don't touch me, bitch!" she spat, sitting up straight in her chair and glowering at Brie.

It was actually good to see the old Mary return.

Master Coen said kindly, "Miss Wilson, we heard you

had an incident today."

She flinched and then looked down in shame. "Yes, Master Coen, but please don't make me talk about it in front of *these* two."

"You will be expected to share what happened with your fellow students. However, not tonight," Master Coen said firmly. Brie could see Mary stiffen in her chair in anger, but she kept silent. "An experienced counselor has been called. You will share with him what happened so that you can pinpoint the exact trigger."

Marquis Gray added, "This mistake does not have to end your training."

Brie was surprised to see tears fall down Mary's cheeks. She choked out, "Thank you, Marquis."

"However, if you ever fail to obey us again, I promise you it will be the last mistake you make," Ms. Clark stated.

Brie pursed her lips. *Good ol' Ms. Clark. Kick ya when you're down.*

Master Coen cleared his throat, sounding annoyed by Ms. Clark's insensitivity. "Miss Wilson, right now we want you to concentrate on being completely open with the counselor."

A short time later, the elevator doors opened and an older gentleman exited. He nodded to the trainers and walked directly to the girls. He held out his hand to Mary, gracing her with a genuine smile. "You must be Miss Wilson. It is a pleasure to meet you. Would you mind talking with me for a bit?"

She meekly took his hand and walked away. As Brie watched her go, a shiver of fear traveled down her spine.

Could that happen to her, too?

As if reading her mind, Marquis Gray said, "It appears Miss Wilson was engaging in an activity that triggered a traumatic reaction based on an unresolved issue in her past. Just as Miss Bennett could have caused a similar situation, had she not informed us of her abuse at the hands of bullies as a child. Without that information, Baron could easily have triggered a negative episode without knowing the cause. I hope you both understand the importance of full disclosure with your Dominants."

The girls nodded. Brie was suddenly grateful for her natural openness. She was surprised Mary had been so stubborn. Sir had asked twice that they go over their journals and take out anything that might cause problems. That girl was her own worst enemy.

Debriefing

Ms. Clark started the panel's discussion. "Even though we don't have Miss Wilson with us, it is imperative we go over your scenes tonight. I'll start with you, Ms. Taylor. How would you rate your experience today?"

Lea grinned. "I would definitely give it a nine. My Dom looked and talked like a real doctor. He even had his room set up to look like an examination room, complete with table, paper gown and chilled air. There were a few times I forgot it wasn't real."

"Excellent. And you, Miss Bennett?"

Brie answered with her eyes cast downward, determined to never look Ms. Clark in the eye again unless the woman specifically asked. "It was a ten. Although there weren't any tepees or feathers, his creativity and thoroughness made it real for me. Just like Lea, there were times that it was so real that it was disconcerting, but I liked that feeling."

"I would expect no less from Rytsar Durov. He has an exceptional reputation." Ms. Clark huffed. "Still can't

believe he lowered himself by fraternizing with a beginner. Miss Bennett, you are lucky he happened to be in
town and—apparently—bored."

"Yes, Ms. Clark."

Brie would have to hang on to Sir's advice to remain
true to herself if she ever met Rytsar again. It would be
hard not to be a bundle of nerves around someone so
well respected in the Dom/sub community.

Ms. Clark returned her attention to Lea. "What was
the main aspect of your encounter that made it a success,
Ms. Taylor?"

Lea shivered in pleasure when she answered. "I loved
the way he experimented with unusual toys and kept
telling me, 'Relax, this won't hurt a bit.' Gives me chills
just thinking about it."

"So there was never a time you were scared or dis-
trustful of your Dom during the scene?"

"Well, I was nervous at times but never scared. Yeah,
I trusted him." She added with a wink, "He was my
doctor, after all."

Ms. Clark remarked dryly, "Don't try to be cute, Ms.
Taylor." Lea nodded her head, properly chastised.

"What about you, Miss Bennett?"

"Well, I about died when I saw the horse and he
took me for a ride on the beach at night. However, I
think what made it real was when he forced me to take
him anally. I wasn't prepared for that and was frightened
at first. I truly felt like a virgin being taken by my warri-
or."

"Yes, Rytsar understands a woman's psyche well,"
Ms. Clark commented, almost wistfully. It made Brie

wonder if Ms. Clark had spent time with Rytsar Durov herself.

Master Coen asked, "Was there anything you found challenging or uncomfortable to obey, Miss Bennett?"

She thought about it and sighed. "Actually, there was one thing. He wanted me to go to the bathroom while he was still in the room. It made me squeamish and I balked at first."

"There should be no hesitation on such a simple request. It's a harmless power play," Ms. Clark admonished. For some reason, Brie suddenly had an image of the Mistress peeing in front of Rytsar, and she struggled not to laugh.

"You need to think on why that caused you to hesitate before obeying your Dom," Marquis Gray told her. "You may dismiss it as nothing, but my experience suggests something deeper is involved."

"I will do as you ask. Thank you, Marquis Gray." He believed in her potential as a submissive and had defended her when others had insisted on her dismissal. She respected Marquis' opinion and was determined to take his advice to heart.

Ms. Clark asked Lea, "Were there any struggles for you, Ms. Taylor?"

"Nope. My Dom was awesome! The way he explained the procedures and what he was going to do with his instruments was so damn sexy. I totally trusted him."

Brie shuddered inside. She hated doctors, and the thought of one sticking anything into her was anything but sexy. Lea was proof that every woman had her own idea of what made the perfect fantasy.

Sir rejoined the panel, but did not sit down. Brie heard the ding of the elevator and knew Tono had left the building. "I would like to talk to each of the girls alone, starting with Ms. Taylor." He turned to her and gave his familiar, "Follow."

Lea popped out of her seat and walked behind him, leaving Brie alone with the three other trainers. Normally, that would have been intimidating, but all Brie could focus on was the fact that she would get time alone with Sir.

The three trainers grilled her on specifics and asked her to rate herself. That proved a difficult question for Brie to answer. She thought back over the entire night and realized she'd pretty much concentrated on enjoying the experience instead of pleasing her Dom. "I guess maybe a six."

"Why that number?" Master Coen asked.

"Well, I know I'm inexperienced, and to be honest, I was having too much fun. I wasn't concentrating enough on my Dom."

"A sub's obvious enjoyment is always appreciated," Marquis Gray stated.

Master Coen disagreed strongly. "But *not* at the expense of the Dom's."

Ms. Clark raised her eyebrow. "We will get an accurate picture of your performance from Rytsar Durov, Miss Bennett. Each Dom fills out a full report on their submissive. By Monday you will know exactly how you rate." The tone of her voice made it clear she thought Brie had overestimated herself.

Marquis Gray stood up and walked over to Brie, then

handed over her fantasy journal. "Look through your entry and tell us which details you experienced today."

She opened her beloved little book, loving it even more now that Rytsar had made its contents come to life. She glanced up and noticed each of the trainers appeared to have a copy of her entry. They had their pens poised and ready, making her wonder what they planned to jot down. It made her nervous.

Brie perused her fantasy before speaking. "Well, like I stated before, he did not look the part of an Indian warrior, but he certainly played the part well. He started the chase as soon as I exited the car, and threatened to cane me if I didn't run." Her nipples hardened as she recalled how fearful she'd been during the chase. "After he caught me, he tied me up and carried me to his 'tepee', where there was a raiding party waiting inside. I remember there was one man in particular who gave me the creeps and kept wanting to touch me. He must have been playing the rival warrior in my fantasy." *Pure genius*, she thought. "My Dom left me alone for hours to hear their celebration. When Rytsar finally claimed me, he took me both vaginally and anally. He forced me to surrender to his desire, but he did it with tenderness like the warrior in my daydreams." She felt the heat building between her legs just talking about it. She glanced up and noticed all three trainers writing furiously.

Brie decided not to mention the interruption by the police. "Since my fantasy pretty much stopped there, he added his own flair by making me come in front of his guests and then commanding me to give him fellatio. But the icing on the cake was when he tied me back up and took me on a horseback ride in the dark where I serviced him again next to a warm fire." She sighed in contentment. "I don't think it gets any better than that. Every part of my fantasy was played out…and then some."

When Master Coen finished with his notes, he stated, "Normally, this is something you would do with your Dom afterwards, especially if it is the first time playing out a scene. It is important to go over the events together so you can let your Dominant know what you found stimulating, and if there was an important element missing or one that should be eliminated altogether."

Brie nodded her head. She knew exactly what she would say to Rytsar if she could. *Please, Rytsar, do it again!*

Sir came back with Lea. He looked over at Brie and nodded before heading back to his office. She stood up, trying to calm her rapidly beating heart. She wanted to look cool and detached for the panel, not like the helplessly devoted sub she was. She followed Sir, listening to his confident stride. It wouldn't take much for her to forget what mattered and give in to her desire for him. Surely, he could feel it.

He gestured her inside, but left the door open this time. She was grateful—and disappointed. She started to kneel, but he stopped her.

"No, Miss Bennett. Sit in the chair."

She moved to the chair, her hands trembling slightly when she grabbed the armrests. She shoved both hands into her lap as soon as she was seated. Brie kept her eyes downcast, afraid her face would express her deep need for him.

"Since I missed out on the discussion, the first thing

I want to ask is how your encounter went today."

She wondered how he would take her honest answer. "It was exceptional, Sir."

"Good. I expected no less. When I mentioned to Durov that I had a unique sub training with us, he offered to evaluate you."

Brie almost glanced up out of shock. *Sir invited Rytsar to bid for me?*

"I had two reasons, really," he continued. "One, I was curious to see if he would agree with my assessment and two, I knew he would provide you with a complete experience." Brie felt the blood rush to her cheeks. "I shall find out tomorrow exactly what he thought, but I am curious as to what you think he will say."

"I'm unsure, Sir."

"It is an easy question, Miss Bennett. Did you serve him well, or not?"

"I did my best, Sir." She thought back to her hesitancy in the bathroom and her freak-out when he'd first tried to take her anally. "However, I remained true to myself."

Sir chuckled with that low, masculine rumble she adored. "I'm glad to hear it. Now, on to the real reason I called you into the room. I want to discuss what happened to Miss Wilson and I need you to look me in the eye."

Brie held her breath and stared into Sir's eyes, becoming completely lost in them the instant she made eye contact.

"Miss Bennett, know that Miss Wilson is getting the best care. I fully expect that she will remain in the program. She was in the hands of a capable Dom who recognized what was taking place."

Brie would have expected no less from Tono.

Sir picked up a pen and started to roll it between his fingers and thumb. She couldn't help it—she imagined those fingers were playing with her nipple in the same manner and felt a gush of wetness between her legs.

"Naturally, seeing one of their comrades in such a state would be disconcerting for anyone. Do you have any questions or concerns?"

Brie swallowed, trying to concentrate on his words rather than his fingers. Her gaze traveled from his hand up to his face, lingering on those firm and commanding lips. She knew their taste and had felt their magic touch on her flesh...

"Miss Bennett."

She quickly stared at her lap again, forcing herself to get a grip. "Naturally, I couldn't help but wonder if it could happen to me, Sir."

"But after talking to the panel?"

"I feel more confident that it won't." She braved another look at him. "Because I'm not one who can hide things."

The intensity of his gaze consumed her. It took everything Brie had not to bow at his feet.

Sir put the pen down slowly and then laced his fingers together. He said in his low, chocolaty voice, "I would agree. Your openness is an asset that will serve you well."

Breathe, girl, breathe. She was imagining his light touch on her skin. Could he read her willingness in her eyes?

194

"Are you worried about Miss Wilson?" he asked.

She shivered a little, because there was something that was bothering her. "Sir, will Mary really be forced to tell us what happened? Shouldn't something that painful be kept private?"

"The three of you must learn from each other. It is part of the strength of this program. Yes, she will share the details from her past that caused her to react so violently tonight, but she will be instructed on how much needs to be revealed. You are a collective now; it is imperative you learn as a unit. Consider it a submissive sisterhood of sorts."

She nodded, not breaking eye contact with him.

His eyes traveled to her collar and she felt a warm burn around her neck. "Anything else you would like to discuss, Miss Bennett?"

Her voice trembled. "Sir, I—"

He put his hand up to stop her. "We must keep to our roles. I am your trainer and you are my student. Your future depends on remembering that."

She blurted it anyway, despite his warning. "I am glad you were my first, Sir."

He looked down at his folded hands and said nothing. Each ticking second that went by broke her confidence. Maybe she had misread his intentions.

"If that is all, you are dismissed. Tell the panel I will join them after I finish the paperwork."

Brie stood up and turned, a single tear falling down her cheek as she walked away. Had she just been a conquest for him? *I'm such a fool.* As she headed towards the door, she straightened her back and lifted her head a little higher.

"Brie." Her name on his lips was like honey.

She turned, discreetly wiping the tear away. "Sir?"

"I am grateful, as well."

"I'm thrilled to hear that, Sir," she whispered.

He nodded, and then picked up the pen on his desk and began to write. She walked down the hallway, trying to contain the utter joy she felt. She concentrated on her walk to calm herself down. The damn heels were starting to feel like a part of her, and she just loved the way they clicked on the tiled floor.

When she returned to the commons, she saw that Mary had rejoined the group. She had a peaceful expression on her face and looked more relaxed than Brie had ever seen her. It was a pleasant look for Mary.

After Brie had delivered Sir's message, she sat down between the two girls. Mary tensed and growled under her breath, in typical Blonde Nemesis fashion.

Marquis Gray stood up. "We have kept you longer than we'd intended due to tonight's unusual circumstances. You have a full day of rest tomorrow. We expect you to take time to reflect on this past week. We will read over your Doms' evaluations and base this coming week's curriculum around what we discover."

He looked at each of the girls, but focused specifically on Brie. Once again, she found his dark eyes penetrating her soul. Was he trying to gauge the extent of her interaction with Sir? She hoped her calm exterior gave nothing away.

His eyes narrowed as if he suspected something, but he didn't comment on it. "We will see you Monday, then.

Come prepared for a thorough critique. You are dismissed—except for you, Miss Wilson. We would like to speak with you privately."

Lea and Brie stood up and smiled at each other. Brie was planning to ask Lea to join her at her apartment for a little nightcap. Maybe Lea would even agree to be filmed and they could both share their individual fantasies for her documentary. One thing was certain, it was going to be a late night, full of girly fun and plenty of giggles.

She looked back at Mary and actually felt a pang of sympathy. That poor woman had suffered through a difficult experience, and now she was being forced to stay after hours to discuss it. It surprised Brie to realize that she cared about the bitch. *Who would have guessed?*

Just as the elevator doors closed, Brie saw Sir sit down with the panel. She held her breath, hoping he would look in her direction, but he didn't. She understood that he couldn't.

Damn, graduation day seemed a lifetime away. She forced herself to concentrate on the week that lay ahead, a week that promised new lessons and a ton of sexy adventures.

Anatomy of the Mighty Shaft

Lea had not left Brie's apartment until four in the morning. They'd been having way too much fun discussing their training experiences to call it a night until it was close to dawn. It had left Brie so exhausted that she'd slept until noon the next day. Her time spent with Rytsar had been an extraordinary gift that still permeated her being the moment she woke. The Russian Dom's take on her warrior fantasy had been something she would cherish forever. It was hard to believe that just a week ago she'd been bemoaning her boring life, but now…life couldn't be more thrilling or challenging.

She got out of bed and immediately bent over in pain. *Oh, crap!* She ran to her calendar and counted out the weeks. Shit, her body was like clockwork. Now what was she going to do? Missing five days of training would be totally unacceptable.

She grabbed her phone and emailed the Submissive Training Center. Thankfully, Rachael answered her an hour later.

Dear Miss Bennett,

Thank you for emailing me about your concern. Rest assured we are quite aware of our students' cycles. If you recall, it was one of the questions on your application. Keep in mind we have been doing this for twenty-five years and have it down to a science. This week's curriculum will not require vaginal penetration.

Your classmates happen to be in sync with each other and are a week later than you, so that week has been planned out as well. (Now you have a better understanding of why we keep the classes quite small.)

You will not miss any training, so I humbly suggest you enjoy your day off and not let it concern you further.

If you have any more questions, please don't hesitate to email or call.

Sincerely,
Rachael Dunningham

Brie felt a surge of relief, but she couldn't help wondering what the week's curriculum would involve if there wasn't going to be any pussy action.

She spent the day pampering herself with the movie *9 ½ Weeks*, a pedicure and Chinese takeout. In the evening, she recorded an addition to her latest training session for the documentary she was making. She specifically addressed her reluctance to obey Rytsar over a simple command, because Marquis Gray had insisted it was important.

Brie looked directly into the lens. "Why was I hesitant? Well…it's so private. I don't know. It felt weird having him stand in the bathroom. I realize it's not *really* a big deal, but I balked. It wasn't until my Dom looked cross with me that I pulled down my panties. I can't tell you how thankful I was when he left the room so my shy bladder could release." She sighed and shrugged. "I guess I just won't think about how exposed I feel if it happens again. Seriously, if my Dom wants to use it as a power play then, just like Ms. Clark said, it's a harmless enough request." Brie snickered at the camera. "Although imagining mean ol' Ms. Clark peeing for Rytsar cracks me up!" She giggled as she turned off the camera.

Monday morning came far too soon. Even though she was looking forward to her evening classes, getting through another tedious day at the tobacco shop was pure torture. There was also the added pressure of knowing they were going to be rated by their weekend Doms. What if Ms. Clark was right and she had highly overrated herself? *Master Coen and Ms. Clark will never let me live it down.*

"Brie, what's wrong with you today?" Mr. Reynolds asked with genuine concern. "You've put all the cigarettes in the wrong spots. You'll have to redo them all."

She gave out an irritated sigh. Stocking the cigarettes wasn't even her job, but Jeff was on vacation in Florida with the owner of the shop. In fact, all of the employees except Mr. Reynolds and Brie were sunning themselves in Florida. She noted it was another reason *not* to hire family when running a business.

She pulled the cigarettes off the shelves and started over, apologizing to him. "I'm sorry, sir… No, I mean, Mr. Reynolds." Brie felt heat rise to her cheeks. Calling anyone else 'sir' felt wrong, no matter how she meant it. He looked at her oddly, but let it pass.

Brie was extremely grateful when her shift was over. She raced home to get ready for class and arrived at the Training Center fifteen minutes early. She was shocked to find Blue Eyes at the entrance of the school, apparently waiting to talk to her. He held out his hand and formally introduced himself. "Hi, my name is Todd Wallace."

She hesitated and did not immediately shake his hand. Seeing him here was disconcerting, considering the last time they'd met he'd called the cops to rescue her from a supposed kidnapping.

He chuckled self-consciously. "I want to apologize again for this weekend. I never meant to embarrass you."

She smiled slightly and took his hand. "That's okay. I appreciate that you were looking out for my welfare."

He seemed relieved and gave her a crooked grin. "I didn't realize there is another school on this campus. So…you're studying to be a submissive?"

She burned with—what? Guilt? Shame? It was the first time someone from outside the school had known what she was doing. Well, she had no reason to feel ashamed, so she answered, "Yes, I am currently enrolled in the Training Center."

"That's great… I mean, I never knew such a thing existed until I checked the website."

She knew exactly what Blue Eyes had found when he'd clicked on the website—all kinds of erotic photos of women in various BDSM poses. The last thing she needed was a total novice thinking he had a chance with her.

"Well, I can't be late for class." She brushed past him and hurried to the elevator.

Mr. Gallant was preparing for his lesson and acknowledged her with a slight nod. She sat down and waited patiently for the bell to ring. Her eyes were riveted to the papers lying on his desk. Those had to be their evaluations. She hoped he would keep the contents of them private, but knowing the school's emphasis on teaching the girls as a unit, she suspected everyone would know how she'd rated with Rytsar Durov.

She let out a nervous sigh and Mr. Gallant glanced up at her. "Anything wrong, Miss Bennett?"

She graced him with a tense smile. "Just curious about my evaluation, Mr. Gallant."

He nodded his head in understanding, but did not relieve her fears by reassuring her.

Both Mary and Lea entered the classroom at the same time. Once they were seated, he began the class—a full five minutes before the bell.

"I know you are all curious to know what your Doms thought of you, so I won't drag it out any longer than necessary. However, I have a question I want you to ponder before you look over your evaluations. Do you believe it is possible to be the *perfect* sub?"

Brie would have answered yes, but the tone in which he'd asked the question made her think it was the wrong answer. *But why couldn't a submissive become the best at everything?* Surely, it had to be possible—it was her single driving goal.

He handed Lea her evaluation first. "Master Harris gave you an overall rating of five. Very good, considering your three days of training. Please look over the individual points so you can identify your strengths and weaknesses."

He walked over to Mary next. "Tono Nosaka chose not to give you a final rating because of your episode. However, he did comment on those elements he experienced with you." If Blonde Nemesis was embarrassed, she sure didn't show it. She took the evaluation and calmly glanced through it.

Mr. Gallant walked over to Brie last. "Miss Bennett, Rytsar Durov gave you a rating of seven. Very unusual considering your level of training and his expertise. Note the areas of weakness and seek to improve on them." She was stunned when he gave her a little wink as he handed the paper over. Mr. Gallant was proud of her, and it thrilled her to no end.

Suck on that, Ms. Clark! she thought. As she studied the evaluation, Brie was humbled by Rytsar's comments. "Great potential. Attractive presentation. An enthusiastic fuck. Played her part well, but with an individual flair." But it was his negative comments that stayed with her. "Resisted a simple command. Severely lacking in oral skills. Ignored her Master in the initial car ride from the school."

Brie burned with shame. She'd always thought she was good at giving head. To be criticized for severely lacking in that department was humiliating. She was also mortified to realize she'd obsessed over Tono purchasing Mary when she should have focused solely on her Dom. It didn't matter whether he had been paying attention to her at the time or not. Rytsar had been right to call her on it.

Mr. Gallant spoke up after giving them several minutes to digest their evaluations. "You were told that we would focus this week's training around your evaluations. After reading through them, it is quite obvious you three are beginners when it comes to oral skills. This week we will have to start with the basics."

Brie actually sighed with relief. *At least we all suck. Well…we suck, but not very well.*

Mr. Gallant took three chairs and placed them at the front of the classroom. "Please join me up here," he instructed.

The girls moved over to the seats. Thankfully, Lea sat in the middle so Brie did not have to sit next to Mary, who was eyeing her with loathing. Mary was obviously jealous of her rating and that made Brie quite happy.

An extremely handsome man with wheat-colored hair and hunky muscles entered the classroom. He immediately stripped out of his clothes before standing before them. Brie couldn't help staring, because the man was mightily endowed.

Mr. Gallant took a small pointer and gave them an anatomy lesson. "Here is a quick list of the sensitive areas of the penis. The slit on the tip of the penis is called the meatus. The corona is the ridge around the head of the penis. The frenulum is the stringy bit just under the head of the cock. The base is just above the testicles. All of these points are highly sensitive and provide maximum stimulation. Naturally, you will need to be aware what is pleasurable and not pleasurable for each Dom." He slid the pointer up and down the man's large dick. "Many women mistake stroking the shaft as adequate stimulation. Although it is an important part of fellatio, the shaft has the least number of nerve endings."

The simple touches of the pointer were having an effect on the model. His large dick was becoming even more impressive.

Mr. Gallant continued, "Massaging the balls can boost the feeling of erection, especially scrunching them gently upwards. Taking the balls into your mouth and sucking lightly will also add to his pleasure. The perineum is the area between the testicles and the anus. Do not forget this area. You can stimulate it with either a finger caress or a lick. Pay particular attention to the amount of pressure your partner enjoys."

He held out the pointer and asked Brie to take it. "Please point out the areas as I name them."

She looked shyly at the model. What did it feel like to be an anatomy lesson for a small group of submissives? Then it struck her. He was a submissive too, no different than they were. It gave her a little more courage when Mr. Gallant told her to point out where the frenulum was. He seemed pleased that she had listened and was able to successfully identify all the body parts as they were called out.

He had her sit down and did the same with the other two girls. Poor Lea was not the studious type and made several mistakes. Mr. Gallant patiently went over the names until she had correctly identified each one. After Lea had sat back down, he dismissed their hunky model. The poor man had to re-dress with his massive hard-on straining against his pants. He left the classroom, walking stiffly. Brie felt for him—sometimes the life of a submissive was not an easy one.

"Ladies, your practicums this evening will test what you have just learned. I expect you will have far more success now you are better acquainted with penis basics. Make good use of your newfound knowledge."

The girls went back to their original seats to collect their belongings. Brie was more than ready to begin the first practicum of the night. However, Mr. Gallant asked them to sit down again.

"You will have homework this week. Please take this home and practice relaxing your gag reflexes." He handed each of them a skin-colored phallus. Brie was frightened by the width and size of it, even though it was only six inches long. "It is flexible, like a real penis, and has been made especially for this practice. You are *not* allowed to use medication to relax your gag reflexes artificially."

Brie looked at it again with trepidation. She'd gagged on a toothbrush while brushing her teeth before. How the heck was she going to take a cock down her throat?

Oral Practicums

T he girls spent the night on their knees, servicing the cocks of unknown Doms. Sir commanded the area to stimulate and whether it was to be with the tongue, lips, teeth, or manual caresses. Her new Dom for the second practicum was of Italian descent. His long, dark hair was tied back in a sexy ponytail. Even better, he had waxed his pubic hair so that she could thoroughly taste and tease all his manly parts. Servicing him was a pleasurable education. She watched him shiver and groan while she experimented with his cock. His body language, guttural noises and hand movements told her exactly what pleased him most.

Ms. Clark—who had been unusually subdued that night—announced at the end of the session, "Unless your Dom says otherwise, assume you will be swallowing his ejaculation. This is an honor."

As if on cue, Brie's Dom began thrusting his cock faster in preparation of his climax. His semen shot into her mouth. She instinctively understood the importance of swallowing his male essence and gulped with enthusiasm, wanting to receive that part of him.

Brie heard one of the other girls gagging, and felt sorry for her—and the Dom. To have his seed rejected was unacceptable. However, she also sympathized with the girl who wanted to take it, but whose body was struggling to accept the taste and consistency. Brie was lucky that the idea of his gift had more than compensated for the bitter taste of her Dom's viscous come. She'd enjoyed connecting with him in such an intimate manner.

Her Italian Dom stroked her hair in appreciation afterwards. She looked up at him and purred, "Thank you."

After the Dom had left the room, Master Coen pulled her aside to talk to her privately. "Miss Bennett, I am sure you are pleased with the rating Rytsar Durov gave you, but I caution you not to let it go to your head. You made several grievous errors as a submissive. What is acceptable as a beginner will be frowned upon later on."

She kept her eyes lowered. "I understand, Master Coen. Trust me, I am upset by my mistakes. I will do my best to overcome them."

"See that you do." He paused for a moment. "I feel it is necessary to tell you that I am still opposed to you remaining in the program, but not because I doubt your abilities."

She looked up at him in surprise. "I don't understand."

"You are causing dissension within the panel. This is not acceptable. The strength of the program depends heavily on the cohesiveness of the trainers. For whatever reason, you are disrupting that."

She looked back down at her lap. "I'm sorry."

"I do not blame you, Miss Bennett. I would simply prefer to be rid of you. However, I do not have the final say. My job is to instruct the students, so I will continue to do so regardless of my preference."

"Thank you, Master Coen."

"No need to thank me," he said irritably, dismissing her for the evening.

As she drove back to her apartment, she wondered if that had been the Dominant's way of apologizing. It made her smile. Apologies did not appear to come naturally to Master Coen.

Brie immediately cleaned the lifelike phallus when she arrived home and attempted to stick it deep into her mouth. She instantly gagged and had to pull it out. There was no way it was going down.

Brie got on the computer and googled how to deep-throat a guy. There were many suggestions, but the one that resonated with her was pretending to yawn to open up her throat. She tried it and sure enough, the phallus went in—but then her throat constricted around it and she freaked. She pulled it out and started coughing, tears running down her face. *Not a comfortable feeling at all!*

She continued her internet search for further tips and came across information on how to eat pussy. Curiosity got the best of her, and she read a researched way to guarantee an orgasm through cunnilingus. *Who knew there were researchers out there studying that kind of thing?* She suspected those nerdy men had probably become quite popular with the ladies after the publication of their unusual research.

Unfortunately, Brie went to bed late, no closer to taking the phallus down her throat. As she undressed, she looked over at her six-inch heels. Those damn things had eventually succumbed to her will. There was no reason she couldn't prevail over a six-inch dildo.

Brie did not wake up with the same confidence the next day, and was relieved that her classes centered on the anatomy of a woman. Brie was amazed to learn the complexity of her own body. Mr. Gallant explained that the glans, the little pea-sized tip of her clitoris, had eight thousand sensory nerve fibers packed into that little button—more than the head of a penis. What astounded her even more was that her clit was only the tip of the clitoris, which had a network of structures within the pelvic region. *Much like an iceberg*, she thought.

Although there was scientific disagreement as to the existence of the G-spot, Mr. Gallant stated his belief that it was part of the clitoral system located at the roof of the vaginal wall, a few inches in. He cited that many women found direct stimulation of the area by either penile or manual manipulation increased the intensity of the orgasm.

The male model from the day before came back into the classroom. "Do I have a volunteer?" Mr. Gallant asked.

Brie had no idea what the large hunk of manhood had to do with female anatomy, but she wanted to find out. She quickly raised her hand, and then put it down— she had momentarily forgotten about her 'condition'. Mr. Gallant called on Nemesis to come to the front of the class.

He asked her to strip off her skirt, panties and corset before sitting on his desk. "Lie back and spread your legs so that your classmates can see the process."

Process? Brie leaned forward, intrigued.

The hunky submissive moved up to Mary and produced a small silver bullet vibrator, similar to the one Brie had at home. Just seeing it caused a tingling in her loins.

Mr. Gallant used his pointer as he spoke. "Most women are unaware of the process their bodies go through as they build up to sexual release. As you can see, at this point Miss Wilson is moderately aroused. You can tell by the slightly engorged outer lips, the pinkening of the entire region and the slickness of the inner lips."

Brie found it both interesting and humorous to be staring at Mary's twat so intently as Mr. Gallant deftly pointed at it.

"As her body is stimulated you will want to note the changes. This will aid you when you are asked to provide cunnilingus." Mr. Gallant nodded at the submissive male.

Brie heard the distinctive sound of the bullet as the sexy hunk switched it on and laid the buzzing toy against Mary's clit. She visibly tensed, before letting out a whimper of pleasure that had Brie shifting in her seat. *What I wouldn't give for a little of that action!*

"Note the erectness of her nipples. As the nipples are stimulated, her body releases oxytocin into her system, which increases her level of pleasure." With that, the sexy sub bent down and started sucking on one of Mary's nipples. Mary moaned loudly as he repositioned the bullet on her clit, and her thighs started to quiver.

"Her respiration is increasing and you can see how the vaginal opening is narrowing. Interestingly, although you can't see it, her inner wall is actually growing in length to accommodate penile penetration. Note, as well, that the clitoris has become erect." Sure enough, Mary's clit was up and begging for more attention. "Notice the color change of the entire area. As the blood concentrates in the groin area, everything swells and darkens. Inside, her G-spot is also engorged with blood and is more sensitive to manipulation."

Mary cried out when the hunk slipped his finger in and starting rubbing her inner spot. She arched her back, pressing her pussy against his hand.

"When the muscular tension reaches a certain level, the body explodes in release."

Mary must have taken it as her cue to let go, because she let out a cry of passion as she came.

The hunk removed his thick finger and Mr. Gallant pointed out, "You can see that the rhythmic contractions of the vagina and sphincter are in sync with one another."

After the last contraction had faded, the hunk helped Mary off the desk. The poor man had another massive hard-on. Brie wondered if he would be left hanging a second time. She hoped not, because she would be more than happy to service him with her mouth.

"Thank you," Mr. Gallant said curtly.

Once more, the hunk was being forced to leave with an aching cock. It seemed so unfair. "Well done," Brie called out. The hunk glanced back and gave her a wink.

She could hear Nemesis purring softly when she sat back down. Brie had to admit it—she was jealous.

The first practicum that night involved Dommes. Interacting with women sexually actually scared Brie. This would be the first time she'd ever eaten pussy and she was terrified of failing. On top of that, being submissive to a female just felt wrong to Brie. She approached her Domme with her gaze glued to the floor and her heart beating rapidly.

Sir began, "I want each of you to take a long lick of your Domme's sex. Get to know and appreciate her taste."

Brie knelt down, took a deep breath and dragged her tongue over the length of the woman's soft, hairless folds. They tasted salty with a tang of musk. *Not unpleasant… I can do this.*

Sir instructed the girls to explore every part of the pussy, first with their fingers and then with their tongues, part by feminine part. From the swollen outer lips to the slick inner lips, the velvety walls inside the vagina and that little sweet spot of nerve endings—the clit.

Eating her Domme was like sampling a part of herself. Brie was nervous and hesitant as she explored the woman's pussy, frightened that she would press or suck too hard and end up hurting her.

Her Domme commanded, "Rub my clit harder, girl.

Bring me to climax."

Brie stopped sucking and used two fingers to flick her clit. The woman put her hand over Brie's and guided her to press harder and flick more vigorously. She watched in fascination as the blood rushed into her Domme's loins, making her outer lips swell in excitement. Brie could feel the heat radiating off her.

The Domme growled softly as her pussy orgasmed under Brie's fingers. She could feel each contraction and her own inner muscles constricted in response to her Domme's pleasure.

"Look at me."

Brie timidly looked up into the green eyes of her Domme. The woman's face was framed by flaming red hair. Brie's eyes widened. She knew this woman. She was the same redhead who had been with Sir in the tobacco shop. Brie was in shock. She'd always assumed the stunning redhead was a submissive, like herself.

"Not bad for a first try, but you need to work on the light touches. It gets irritating after a while."

"Yes, Mistress." Brie bowed her head, relieved it was over. At least she'd succeeded in bringing her Domme to climax.

Ms. Clark Learns a Lesson

B rie was thrilled with herself. Even though she was a newbie, she'd made a female come. *That totally counts as success!*

Not according to Ms. Clark. "Miss Bennett, you looked as if you don't own a cunny of your own. I would have sworn by the way you were eating her that you were a prepubescent boy."

Brie blanched. Mary snickered behind her, but Master Coen heard this time. "Miss Wilson, such an outburst is not permitted. On your knees, now!"

He got up and walked over to her. He grabbed her chin roughly, forcing her to look up at him. "Next time I will slap you in the stockade for an hour. Do you understand?"

She nodded with difficulty, her chin still in his tight grasp. He let go of her and walked back to his seat. Brie felt a burst of gratitude towards Master Coen.

Marquis Gray spoke up. "Ms. Clark, I can't help but notice that you were not as critical of Ms. Taylor's first experience with cunnilingus."

"Ms. Taylor did not have the benefit of Mr. Gallant's instruction. Miss Bennett has no excuse."

Sir addressed her coolly. "As you know, they only went over basics today. Perhaps you feel you could do a better job of training her?" he challenged.

Brie's stomach churned at the thought of touching Ms. Clark. She shuddered unconsciously and prayed the conversation would end. It was totally okay with Brie if Ms. Clark thought she was a failure.

"In fact, I would like to see it. On the stage…right now," Sir stated.

Ms. Clark looked as horrified as Brie felt, but Sir was the headmaster. How could the trainer say no? "Fine."

The panel and the group of girls got up and made their way to the auditorium. Brie was literally shaking as she walked to her doom. Lea put her arm around her in support and gave a little squeeze, as if to say, 'You can do this.'

While everyone else found their seats, both Ms. Clark and Brie made their way up on the stage. Brie started a quick conversation with herself. *Okay, this is my Mistress. I love my Mistress. I would do anything to please her. I love everything about her—her smell, her taste, the sound of her voice, the demands she makes on me… Basically, I love her like I love Sir. Yes, that's it! She is Sir to me right now.*

Ms. Clark asked for a chair, and an assistant immediately produced one. She sat down and asked Brie to stand before her. Brie kept her eyes on the floor and moved within two feet of the woman. Ms. Clark said nothing.

She must still be in shock, too.

"Would you like me to strip, Mistress?" Brie offered, remembering it was the first thing she had asked Lea to do when they had been on stage.

"No. I am not interested in your body."

She'd clearly meant it as an insult, but not having to strip was a gift. It made Brie feel less vulnerable.

"Get on your knees and give me cunnilingus. I have to judge how bad you are before I can help you."

Brie got down on her knees, slowly and gracefully. She pushed up Ms. Clark's tight business skirt. Then she gently peeled off the trainer's black lace thong and spread her Domme's legs apart.

Ms. Clark was a true blonde, with an attractively trimmed snatch. If Brie had had any feelings for females, she might have fallen in love with that pristine pussy.

She closed her eyes and went over the information she'd read on the internet.

Step one—prolong the first lick.

Brie began by lightly kissing the insides of the thighs, then running her fingers gently through the hair on Mistress's mound. It was all about sensually drawing out the first moment before contact. She lightly pressed her mouth against the right side of Mistress' outer lips, and then on the left. Brie ever so lightly kissed the area of her opening and breathed warm air on her clit without touching it. Then Brie took a deep breath and licked the full length of her, from the vaginal opening all the way up. She purred softly after she broke contact, slowly licking Mistress again with more pressure, remembering the redheaded Domme's advice. Brie avoided the clit, wanting it to become desperate for her mouth.

Step two—wait for the clit to show itself and then tease it.

She continued the sensual licking until the glans peeked out from behind the hood. It was Brie's cue to suck lightly on it. Then she pulled away and started licking the length of her Domme's sex again, coming close to the clit but not always suckling it, making Mistress anticipate and long for more contact.

Step three—use your fingers to stimulate. She started playing with Mistress' glistening folds and teased her opening with her fingers. Then, when Brie felt the time was right, she slowly penetrated her with a single finger. She played with the opening and then explored farther in to find the G-spot. Mistress shuddered when Brie found it.

Step four—use your tongue to build the tension.

Brie started to concentrate on the glans, using a horizontal fluttering of her tongue as she stroked her Domme inside. She switched it up by tilting her head to one side and then the other. When her tongue got tired, she laid it flat on the clit and let Mistress grind against it. Brie remembered reading that two fingers were better than one, so she slipped another finger in to thoroughly caress the G-spot.

Mistress moaned. Not a quiet, controlled moan. No, this was the moan of a woman coming close to the edge. Brie pressed her mouth against her Domme's clit and licked with a steady, sensual pace as she used her other hand to caress the soft skin just under the vagina.

Step five—stimulate other sensitive areas to bring her over the edge.

The moans grew louder and Mistress shifted in the chair. Brie remembered how possessed she'd felt when both Sir and Rytsar had taken her anally. With confidence she hadn't had until that moment, Brie moved her finger down to Mistress' anus and teased the rim. When the timing felt right, she inserted her finger into the tight hole.

Mistress cried out and started orgasming on Brie's tongue. It was exciting for Brie to experience success with such a difficult partner. She continued to lick lightly until she felt Mistress' hand on her head. She pulled away and looked to the floor, very pleased with herself but trying not to show it.

"What the hell was that?" Ms. Clark asked hoarsely.

"Miss Bennett," Sir called from the panel.

Brie stood up and wiped her mouth. "Sir?"

"Can you explain how a supposed novice employs advanced cunnilingus techniques?"

She looked up at him and said simply, "I googled it, Sir."

All three men broke out in laughter. She blushed and looked down at the stage floor.

After the laughter had subsided, Sir asked Ms. Clark, "Well? Are you satisfied with her cunnilingus skills?"

Her trainer adjusted her skirt before answering. "I am satisfied for now."

Brie heard manly chuckles coming from the panel as she made her way off the stage. *Thank God for the internet*, she thought.

Lea gave her hand a squeeze. The encouragement shining in her eyes made Brie smile inside. She had accomplished what she'd thought was impossible. She'd made Ms. Clark climax—and loudly, at that.

Facing the Challenge

That night, Brie practiced with the dildo again. Because of her experience with Ms. Clark, she'd discovered the secret to helping her overcome her gag reflex. This time, she brought the dildo to her mouth and thought of Sir.

Sir wanted to take her orally; he longed to feel her throat caress his shaft. Brie concentrated on her vision of Sir as she pressed the head against the back of her throat. She broke through the resistance and felt it slide down. It was a strange feeling and she immediately pulled it back out. She coughed a little, but nothing like she had the night before.

Brie took it again. This time when it slipped in, she pushed in farther and left it there. She couldn't breathe, but she'd anticipated that and it did not frighten her.

This time, when she pulled the phallus out, it was covered in thick saliva. Thicker than she'd seen before. She'd read that was normal, but she cleaned it off because it grossed her out. She pushed the phallus down her throat again and this time she gently, with the tiniest of movements, thrust the shaft back and forth deep in her throat. She could just imagine how good it felt to Sir. He was groaning in pleasure. She pulled back out to breathe, but then she went right back and began the gentle thrusting.

Sir played with her hair and growled huskily. "That's it, Brie. Love my cock with your throat," he groaned.

She did just that. Brie kept taking it deeply, caressing the head with her tight orifice. She imagined him grabbing her head to stop the motion as he came. When she pulled away, she looked up into his eyes and saw lust mixed with love.

She went to bed satisfied. She'd conquered the six-inch cock faster than the damn shoes. Nothing was going to stand in her way of becoming the best sub the Training Center had ever seen.

The first practicum the next evening was a wonderful treat. Brie was thrilled to see Baron waiting for her. It seemed as if it had been ages since their last encounter. She was pleased to note that he seemed equally excited to see her.

"Kitten, it has been a while," he stated, tilting her head up and leaning down to kiss her.

She gazed into his hazel eyes and smiled. Brie pressed her mouth against his thick lips, breathing in his spicy musk. It felt like a homecoming. She'd changed a great deal since that first night, when she'd been frightened and he'd been the one to guide her through a difficult scene. "I've missed you," she whispered.

Sir spoke to the group. "Tonight you will be deep-throating your Doms. Mr. Gallant instructed you to practice relaxing your gag reflexes. We expect you've taken the time to accustom your throats to penetration."

Brie snuck a quick glance up at Baron and grinned. Even though he wasn't Sir, he was a Dom she would enjoy pleasing.

"For this first practicum, you will be in control of the movement. Take your time; don't feel you need to rush. We understand this is the first time for each of you."

When Baron gave the command, Brie knelt down on the floor and unzipped his pants. She pulled down his briefs as well and helped him to step out of them. She didn't want clothing to be a distraction.

Even though his cock was thicker than the dildo she had practiced with, she was confident she could take it into her throat. She began by stroking his chocolaty cock. She licked and nibbled the head, glancing up at him every now and then to see his reaction. Baron stared down at her lustfully and stroked her long curls.

She began taking more and more of him into her mouth. She teased his manhood, hoping to make him wonder when she would make that final push. She grasped his balls and kneaded them gently as she twisted her mouth around his cock farther, stimulating his sensitive head.

When she felt the time was right, she grabbed onto his hips with both hands and slowly pushed his cock to the back of her throat. She made the motion of yawning and felt the head breach the entrance. For a second she balked, but she resisted the urge to pull away and pushed her lips to the base of his cock. Then she pulled out slowly and took a deep breath.

"Oh, kitten, I like…very much," Baron growled.

She looked up at him and smiled. She took his cock again, this time determined to press her lips against his groin. When she felt the tickle of his pubic hair, she silently congratulated herself. She started the gentle thrusting deep in her throat and heard him groan loudly.

She pulled away to take another breath. This time, he gathered her hair in his hand so he could watch the action. As she took him again, she kept her eyes on his face. Her lips slid down the entire length of his shaft and pressed against his groin. She felt his whole body shiver as she thrust his cock deep into her throat.

"That looks and feels fucking fantastic," he growled with a low rumble.

Her loins contracted in pleasure at the knowledge that he was enjoying it so much. She continued the process of taking the fullness of his cock, rocking gently against it and then pulling out.

Finally, he could take no more. "I'm going to come deep in your throat, sex kitten."

She pulled his cock out, covered in her thick saliva. She said hoarsely, "I want you to, Baron. I've never felt that before."

He grunted lustfully and gathered her hair again before commanding, "Do it."

She took a couple of deep breaths before opening her lips. Again, she kept her eyes on him as she took his manhood as deep at it would go. This time she rocked his cock a little less gently, causing her throat muscles to tighten around him. He grabbed both sides of her head and cried out as his cock spasmed inside her. His orgasm seemed to last forever. She almost pushed away to get some air, but he released his hold and she was able to breathe again. She was gasping, and she sat on her heels, feeling weak from the endeavor. Instead of pulling her up, Baron knelt down beside her and stroked her cheek with his thumb. "That was artfully done, kitten. You are truly unique."

She looked at him gratefully, feeling a little embarrassed as she wiped away the copious amounts of saliva from her face. "Thank you, Baron. It was my honor."

He stood up and dressed himself as she listened to Lea finishing. It sounded like she was still struggling with the gag reflex, although she didn't let it stop her. Once she had finished and the Doms had exited the room, Sir asked them to face the panel.

"Miss Bennett, once again you surprise us. For a woman who has not taken a shaft down her throat before, you appeared quite comfortable with the act."

She couldn't tell him that he was her inspiration, so she kept it simple. "I've been practicing every night, Sir. I did not want to fail."

Marquis Gray spoke up, "The way you did it was unusually sensual. Where did that come from?"

"I tried to make it pleasurable for my Dom."

His eyes narrowed. "No, there's something more to it. Something I can't quite put my finger on." Brie blushed, hoping he wouldn't figure out that when she had been deep-throating Baron, she'd also been thinking of Sir.

"Whatever the case, it was impressive, Miss Bennett," Master Coen stated. "I really have no criticism."

Naturally, Ms. Clark added her two cents. "I am curious. You did an excellent job with a slow, shallow thrust. I wonder, however, how you will fare when it gets a little rougher."

Brie nodded her head, unsure how to respond.

The other girls' critiques were not as kind. Brie would have silently celebrated her success, except for the fact that Ms. Clark's words resonated in her head. Brie really didn't know how she would handle it. In all her practice, she'd never tried to take the phallus hard and fast. Just the thought of it made her blood run cold.

Pride Before the Fall

Sir informed the trio, "You may proceed to the commons. We will retrieve you in a half-hour. Because of the nature of your second practicum, only liquid refreshments will be served."

The girls remained silent as they walked down the halls. It was quite different from their normal chatting sessions. Of course, their sore throats certainly didn't encourage witty banter.

Brie was grateful to see a nice selection of wine. She grabbed a bottle of Merlot and a glass and sat down at a table. Lea joined her with a couple of bottles of beer. Even Mary came over and sat down at the table. She'd chosen to mix herself a rum and Coke.

After a couple of sips, Mary shocked Brie by saying, "Okay, my doc says I have to share it with you so I'm just going to get it over with."

Brie put her glass down and looked at her sympathetically.

"No! Pick that damn glass up and don't you dare look at me."

Brie glanced over at Lea, but said nothing. She picked up her glass of wine and stared at the opposite wall.

"Neither of you are allowed to say a word. I'm just going to say what I have to say and then I don't want to hear you ever mention it again. Do you understand?" Mary growled.

Both Lea and Brie nodded without looking at her.

"Long story short, my mom abandoned me when I was eight. The bitch just up and left without a goodbye or anything. My dad...he was never parent material. He kind of lost it after she abandoned us." Mary paused, probably contemplating how much to share. "I was left to fend for myself and I did okay on my own. But my dad never got over her leaving and he hated me for it. I could tell by the way he glared at me."

Mary stopped and took a long drink. She seemed about to speak, but then she took another long sip. Brie felt for her and sincerely wished Mary didn't have to reveal her painful past.

"So... By the time I was ten, my dad was heavily into drugs and drank all the time. But the only time it affected me was when he drank his rum and Coke and smoked crack." She stopped again and drank over half of her cocktail. It surprised Brie that Mary would prefer rum and Coke when it'd had such a negative impact on her life.

Mary continued, "The combination did something to his brain and he changed." She barked angrily, "He never touched me sexually, if that's what you're thinking."

Nobody said a word, so she went on, "My dad would

227

make me lean against a kitchen chair and then he'd rant about how he wasn't ever going to let me leave. That's when the beatings would start. He knew exactly where to hit so that it caused the greatest amount of pain without leaving a mark. I think he got off on hearing me scream." Mary picked up her glass and downed the rest of the drink. She got up and made herself a new one.

When she sat down again, she said off-handedly, "A guy would have to think about that, wouldn't he? Where to hit a little girl so it didn't leave a permanent mark? Even though he was drunk and high, I always suspected he was coherent on some level. He just fucking hid behind the drugs and alcohol as an excuse to hurt me."

Brie took a sip of her wine, finding it hard not to turn and give Mary a hug.

"Can you imagine beating up a ten-year-old kid? I fucking hate him! Hell, I hate my mother just as much. He probably got his jollies beating on her too, but what kind of mother leaves her little girl behind with such an animal? I blame her every bit as much as my dad." She mumbled into her drink, "They can both go to hell."

She stopped talking and slowly downed the rest of the drink. Lea asked softly, "What happened last week?"

"Oh, that? Well, Tono has this weird way of tying people up. I liked it at first, but I don't know... It was creepy. I think that's what started it. The two of us were having a good time together. I mean he is a hot piece of ass and God, he can make a girl come. But after being tied up for so long, I started to hyperventilate. He asked if I was okay, but I didn't want to stop so I claimed it was turning me on. He made a fine interrogator and we were just ramping up to the good stuff."

She sighed heavily. "Tono threatened to hurt me un-less I divulged more information. I told him where to go and he slapped my face like in my fantasy. Normally, I like that kind of thing but I just flipped out and started screaming hysterically. I don't even remember what happened after that." No one spoke when she'd finished.

Mary was a mystery to Brie. *Drinking the same drink as her abusive father and seeking out situations similar to the abuse she suffered as a child?* It was almost as if Mary were a moth, drawn to the flame that would eventually burn her.

The more Brie reflected on it, the more she believed it was good that Mary had come to the Training Center. With the help of her counselor and the guidance of the trainers, maybe she would find a Dom who could help her to overcome the demons of her past in a construc-tive way.

Master Coen came soon after to collect them. In-stead of heading to the auditorium, they walked back to the same classroom. When she entered, she saw her hot, Italian Dom waiting for her. She smiled, remembering how smooth and tasty his cock was.

Marquis Gray stood up to address the girls. "To be well-rounded submissives, you should be able to take a good face-fucking. Many Doms enjoy it. For your second practicum, we will observe how well you become vessels for your Doms."

Brie froze. It was one thing to take a man's cock on her own terms and have control of the action, but it was completely different to let him have free rein over her resistant throat.

"Kneel down before your Doms," Marquis Gray ordered.

Brie did so slowly, with a growing feeling of dread.

Her dark-haired Italian commanded, "Undress me, slave."

She undid his pants and pulled them off. His beautiful cock stood before her. She realized it was the exact same size as the dildo. It gave her a little more confidence. She looked down the line and noticed all three men were the same size. *How thoughtful of the trainers to pick normal-sized cocks for our first face-fucking session.*

Brie took her Dom's cock in her hand and began kissing and licking his shaft. He grabbed the back of her head and pushed her mouth farther down on his dick. She adjusted and sucked harder, trying to build up the extra saliva needed to make it easier on her throat. After an ample amount of time, he pushed his cock against the back of her throat.

She gagged and instinctually braced her hands against his thighs, pulling away with tears stinging her eyes.

"Open," he commanded.

She mentally prepared herself for the onslaught and opened her mouth to him. Again, he grabbed the back of her head and forced the length of his shaft down her throat. It wasn't even a choice for her; she pushed against him and broke contact. It hurt.

She turned her head and watched Mary calmly taking the thrusting of her Dom, her face a picture of peaceful acceptance. It was almost beautiful to watch as his dick disappeared into her mouth, again and again in rapid thrusts.

Brie was determined to please her Dom that way. She put her hands behind her back and opened her mouth wide. After two of his forceful thrusts, her hands snaked around of their own accord and tried to push him away.

"Hands," he warned.

She dropped them down to her sides, but the next deep thrust had her pushing against him desperately.

"Hands!"

Her arms hung in midair as she used all the willpower she possessed not to disengage. The tears fell and sobs escaped each time he thrust in and out of her. She could have used the safe word, but she refused, not wanting to fail in this.

She closed her eyes and endured. It was ugly. There was nothing sensual about how she took his shaft down her throat. Her nose was running and she couldn't stop crying. He took pity on her and pulled away. She could only curl up over her knees and attempt to quiet her whimpers.

"Miss Bennett, please follow me," Sir said, standing beside her.

She looked up, all snot-nosed and teary. She tried unsuccessfully to stifle the sob that erupted from her lips. He held out his hand and she took it.

Brie meekly followed him out of the classroom and they walked to his office in silence. He guided her to the chair and then sat down at his desk. He handed her several tissues and waited until she had control over herself.

"Why didn't you use the safe word?" he asked quietly.

"I won't give up. I can't fail."

"But you did just now." The truth of his words crushed her. "I have always told you to be true to yourself. This was a prime example of what I was talking about. By stubbornly enduring it, you have harmed yourself and lessened the chance of becoming successful at this skill."

She looked at him sadly and then broke into a fresh set of tears. "I'm sorry, Sir. I can't stand failing."

"In this case, you failed miserably. We didn't stop you, because we all wanted to see you take control of the situation. Imagine doing something similar, or worse, on your own and then being permanently scarred by it. There is a reason we give you a safe word. What you failed to do is similar to the mistake Miss Wilson made. Do *not* let your stubbornness or pride keep you from ending a scene that is traumatizing you—ever."

Her tears had stopped by then. Now she only felt shame. "I'm sorry, Sir."

"Marquis Gray is correct; most Doms will expect to take you in that manner. It is important you overcome your fear of it."

She nodded despondently.

"Brie." Her stomach fluttered when she heard hearing Sir say her first name. "What if I tell you that I want you that way?"

She looked up at him, and her heart nearly stopped beating.

"I want to feel the tight constriction of your throat

around my shaft. I want to see you look up at me with adoration as I pump my cock into your mouth."

Suddenly the act did not seem as frightening. If it was something Sir wanted, she would willingly give it to him, or at least try.

"Tomorrow, you and I will practice on stage. It is important to succeed in this, but if it becomes too much, say the safe word and you can attempt it again another time." He looked at her kindly. "This does not have to be conquered in one session."

"I want to try, Sir," she said breathlessly. "I want to please you."

"It's only natural. You're a sub."

"No, it's more than that…"

"Stop, Miss Bennett." Her heart ached when he called her by her last name. "Let's not mistake this for anything more than a practice session."

She looked at her lap and answered quietly, "Yes, Sir."

Regardless of his warning, she coveted the chance to please him, to show him how she truly felt. If he knew the extent of her feelings, how could he ever let her go? Sir would never find anyone else as devoted. He was her everything.

She left the Center after their talk and headed straight home. As Brie lay in bed that night, she thought of Sir. *He's probably wondering how I'm doing, or maybe he is imagining my lips wrapped around his perfect cock.* Despite Brie's failure during the second practicum, she longed for this session with Sir. He hadn't really touched her since their encounter together, and she *craved* Sir's touch.

Pleasing Sir

T he next morning at the tobacco shop, Mr. Reynolds noted the extra spring in her step. "Wow, what's got you glowing like a candle?"

Brie blushed and smiled, but said nothing.

"Ah, must be young love. That would explain your lack of focus this past week. Is he the one who gave you that quirky necklace?"

Brie caressed her thin, black collar and said proudly, "Yes."

"So, who is he?" Mr. Reynolds pressed.

She grinned. "Nobody you would know."

He grabbed the inventory sheet and called back to her as he walked away, "You should bring him over to the shop sometime. I'd like to meet the young man who has captured your heart."

She giggled to herself. She could only imagine the look on Mr. Reynolds' face if she came walking into the shop dressed in her sexy school uniform, arm in arm with Sir. The poor man might have a heart attack.

She laughed her way through the day, surprised at

how fast work went when Sir was on her mind. Before she knew it, she was heading to the Training Center and her practice session with the headmaster.

Brie was disheartened to see Blue Eyes—Todd—waiting for her at the front doors again. She hated to be rude to the boy, but it was a necessary evil. He needed to understand that she wasn't interested in him.

"Good evening, Miss Bennett." He swung the door open for her and let Brie pass without trying to engage her in conversation.

Well, that went easier than expected. She snuck a peek to see if he was watching her, but he was talking with another student. She figured he must have gotten the hint the first time around. *Huh, he's smarter than I gave him credit for.*

Brie struggled to pay attention in Mr. Gallant's class, but her mind was intent on pleasing Sir. Her instructor noticed and called her on it. "Miss Bennett, what are the five suggested techniques to enhance fellatio for the male?"

She did a quick replay in her mind. Although she hadn't been paying attention, luckily her mind had taken note and she was able to rattle them off. She held up five fingers and folded each one down as she named the techniques. "One, remain partially dressed. Two, position yourself so that your Dom can see your lips on his cock at all times. Three, continually make sensual sounds. Four, intensify the act physically…"

"Examples?" he asked.

"Um…" Brie was scrambling, but it quickly came to her. "Examples are like having him put his hand on the back of your head or using your hair during fellatio."

"Fine. Go on."

"Five…" She put the last finger down and smiled. "Saliva is your friend."

"That is correct." He looked at her knowingly. "I suggest you employ those techniques tonight."

Was he aware of her upcoming practice session with Sir?

"I will, Mr. Gallant. Thank you."

"Ladies, tonight you will proceed to the auditorium first so that refreshments can be served afterwards."

Her heart rate shot up. She was going to encounter Sir sooner than she'd thought! It was hard not to run to the auditorium. Instead, she walked alongside Lea, who seemed in no hurry whatsoever. Brie almost squealed when she saw that not only were the trainers already there, but Sir was on stage.

"Proceed to the stage, Miss Bennett," Sir commanded with his velvet voice.

She floated to him. It was just Sir and her—there was no other reality.

"Are you ready, Miss Bennett?"

Keeping her eyes on the floor, she responded, "I am, Sir." She paused and added, "Mr. Gallant suggested I use the techniques I learned today."

"Of course. I assumed you would."

She didn't know if it was overly bold, but she asked, "May I strip for you, Sir?"

He snapped his fingers and one of the assistants produced a chair. Sir sat down and graced her with one of his delicious smirks. "By all means."

Brie swayed her hips from side to side, trying to lure Sir into her seductive web. She slowly untied her corset, letting it open, but not allowing it to expose her breasts. Before she undid the last tie, she turned around and looked over her shoulder at him as her corset fell to the floor. She covered her breasts with her arms, her milky white skin blushing with excitement as she turned back towards him. She gave him a sexy pout and then let her hands drop to her sides.

She playfully fingered her long, brown curls and twirled once for him. Then she shimmied out of her panties, held them up and, with a naughty little smile, let them drop to the floor. She briefly lifted her skirt to show off her bare pussy. Next, she removed her shoes and then her hose, one luscious leg at a time. She let the it drift to the floor, on top of her small pile of clothing. She kept her microskirt on, in accordance with the first technique.

Brie approached Sir and slowly knelt down at his feet, ready to take his cock in the position recommended in the second technique. Sir's smile had grown wider as he'd observed her.

"Entertaining to watch," he complimented. He stood up and removed all of his clothes. She marveled at his fit frame, the dark patch of hair on his chest and his princely cock. Then he stood before her, his handsome manhood just inches from her face.

"I want you to suck me the same way you did Baron."

Tears of gratitude pricked her eyes. She was being given permission to express her feelings for him before the practice session. Brie took his rigid and perfectly formed cock in her hand, guiding it to her lips. She swirled her tongue over the ridge of his smooth head and moaned softly, remembering the third technique.

Brie took her time as she took more and more of him into her mouth, building up the anticipation of when her lips would encase his entire shaft. She continually snuck glances at Sir and made lusty noises. He met those glances with his intense stare. He remained silent, but seemed completely entranced by her mouth.

When she felt ready, she looked up at him, hoping her honey-colored eyes clearly expressed her total and complete devotion. The head of his cock breached the entrance of her throat and she slowly forced it down until her lips touched the base of his shaft. Then she grabbed his hips and began the gentle, shallow thrusting motions. Sir threw back his head and let out a deep sigh.

When she needed oxygen, she slowly pulled away, but did not release his cock from her lips. She remembered the fourth technique and guided one of his hands to the back of her head. She purred at the feeling of submissiveness the simple contact inspired. Then she let his hard cock slide back down her tight throat. She began the thrusting motion with a little more enthusiasm. This time Sir groaned in pleasure and a wave of wetness coated her aching pussy. Pleasing Sir was such a turn-on!

She continued loving his cock with her throat. The saliva built up until it was freely flowing from her mouth, but she did not wipe it away—technique number five. She knew it would increase his pleasure, providing his cock with the right amount of friction.

Brie wanted to continue forever, but he finally pulled away and stated, "I want to fuck your face now."

Her loins contracted in pleasure and fear. An assistant entered the stage and handed Sir a strip of red satin. He looked down at Brie tenderly. "I don't want your hands to be a distraction for you this time."

Sir tied her wrists together behind her back. She was grateful. Not having control of her hands would allow her to focus better. He stood before Brie again, his cock stiff and hungry for her.

"Open yourself to me."

She trembled. The way he said it was sexy and romantic. He wasn't treating her like a hole to be fucked; he was asking her to give a part of herself.

"If it pleases you, Sir," she whispered hoarsely. She opened her lips to his manhood.

He gathered her hair with one hand and used it to guide her onto his cock. He gradually forced her mouth farther down his shaft. "First I'll start off gentle, and then I'll give it to you rough."

Brie moaned. Sir was going to take her in the same manner he'd taken her anal virginity. He knew what her body could handle and would help her to succeed in pleasing him. She relaxed as he pushed the head of his shaft against her throat. Brie unconsciously gagged, but did not fight when he forced it past the resistance. She felt the length of him travel down her throat until her lips touched the base of his cock. He slowly pulled back out and let her catch her breath.

"Color?" he asked.

"Green."

He nodded and pushed himself deep into her throat again. He stayed still for a moment, and then thrust lightly several times before pulling out.

"Still okay?" he asked.

She nodded, realizing she wasn't making any noises. This time, when he guided himself down her throat, she gave a muffled moan and looked up at him lustfully. He took that as an okay to thrust with more vigor, and she instinctually tensed.

I am his vessel, she reminded herself. *I long to please him this way.* His thrusts became longer and more forceful. Brie kept her eyes locked on him as he took her mouth for his pleasure, but she forgot to make noises of desire, so he pulled out.

"Color?"

She managed to croak, "Still green."

"Then I won't hold back any longer."

"Thank you, Sir."

He regathered her hair. "Open wide, Brie. I plan to thoroughly enjoy that throat of yours."

Brie remembered the erotic vision of Mary deep-throating her Dom with a look of peace on her face. She wanted to look just as erotic for Sir, but it was so much more than that. She was not offering herself as a vessel to him out of obedience, she was offering herself out of devotion and… She could no longer deny it. Brie gazed up at Sir with *love* as he used her mouth to satisfy his lustful desires.

Sir groaned and eventually cried out. His whole body shuddered when the release finally came and he pumped his essence down her throat. For an instant, she saw a hint of the same vulnerability in his eyes she'd seen before, and it thrilled her.

He untied her hands and helped her to her feet. "You did quite well, Miss Bennett." He re-dressed and then assisted with her clothing, pulling the corset tight. She looked up to thank him and was struck dumb. His lips were nearly touching hers…

Sir put his hands on her shoulders and turned her around to face the panel.

"How would you rate the experience, Miss Bennett?" Master Coen asked.

It was a ten; it would always be a ten with Sir. However, she could not tell the trainers that without causing problems, so she answered, "It was an eight."

"That is a marked improvement from your previous experience," he noted. "We were distressed when you failed to use the safe word the first time."

Brie looked down at the stage floor in shame. "I've learned my lesson, Master Coen."

"One can only hope that's the case."

"What was the difference from yesterday to today?" Marquis Gray asked.

She tried to keep her face emotionless when she answered. "I'm learning better how to give control away."

"That *is* an expected quality in a submissive, Miss Bennett," Ms. Clark interjected.

Marquis Gray's voice had a serious undertone when he said, "Based on my observations, I believe what happened yesterday is closely related to your reluctance to eliminate in front of Rytsar Durov. Can you identify the connection?"

She braved a look into his dark, cavernous eyes, suddenly unsure of herself. "No, I don't see the similarity."

His eyes softened briefly. "I could tell you, but that would not be wise. You must learn to identify your weaknesses so that you can properly address them."

Brie's heart sank. Even though she had conquered the oral skill of deep-throating, Marquis Gray was claiming she still had a weakness—a weakness that threatened her future as a submissive.

"Think long and hard on this, Miss Bennett. If you fail to identify it, I'm afraid it will defeat you."

A chill traveled down her spine. "I will do as you say, Marquis Gray."

"I have faith in you," Sir whispered, putting his hand on the small of her back as they walked off the stage. The simple gesture and his words of encouragement set her heart pounding again.

Auction: The Doctor is In!

B rie was far less nervous on her second Auction Day. After having such an amazing experience with Rytsar Durov the week before, she was confident she would thoroughly enjoy herself. Mr. Gallant had informed the girls that they would be playing out their Doms' fantasies this time around.

She was certain Tono would bid for her and she was looking forward to alone time with the captivating Dom. Even though they'd only had one encounter together, it was one she couldn't forget. They had a special connection she hoped to explore further. Much to her relief, her monthly 'condition' had played out and wouldn't affect her time with him.

When her name was called, Brie walked gracefully onto the stage with her gaze glued to the floor. Ms. Clark would have no reason to discipline her this time around.

The announcer said loudly, "Miss Bennett is twenty-two with a bachelor's degree in filmmaking outside these walls. Her trainers describe her as a quick learner." *Quick learner—now, that's more like it!* That was tons better than last time, when she had been labeled 'difficult'. Brie silently wondered if Sir had had something to do with it.

Although Brie did not look up, she could sense that Tono wasn't in the room. Her heart sank as the bidding started and she didn't hear his warm voice among the crowd. There was no bidding war like the one she had experienced the first time and before she knew it, the announcer called out, "Going once... Going twice... Sold to Master Harris for five hundred dollars."

Brie almost peed her panties. Master Harris had bid on Lea the week before. He had a fetish for the doctor/patient scenario—and Brie *hated* doctors.

She trembled as he came up to her. She studied him out of the corner of her eye. He was handsome in a clean cut, all-American sort of way—six feet tall with a swimmer's build, chestnut hair, and green eyes. He even had cute dimples to go with it. Master Harris took her arm and she walked quietly beside him, trying to keep her fear from showing on her face.

It was one thing to live out a favorite fantasy. It was quite another to live out someone else's fantasy, especially when that fantasy was disturbing to her. She stood meekly by as Lea was auctioned off to a Dominatrix named Mistress White and Mary to a man named Sir Edwards. Poor Mary only received one bid, for two hundred dollars. Brie felt embarrassed for her and wondered if Mary's 'episode' had gotten around to the other Doms.

Master Harris interrupted her thoughts by leaning over and whispering, "I hear you are frightened of doctors. I want you to know that turns me on."

Her lips quivered, but she nodded in response and followed him out of the Center. During the car ride, she remembered to face her Dom, even though she did not stare directly at him. Unlike Rytsar, who'd had an entourage, Master Harris drove his own car. However, it was a Lexus, which totally fit his doctor persona.

"When was the last time you were at the doctor's?" he asked.

Brie answered hesitantly, "A year ago."

"You are definitely due for a complete examination."

Her gut twisted. She reminded herself that Lea had loved this fantasy and had given this Dom a nine out of ten. *It can't be all that bad, right?*

He pulled up to a small but classy house on the side of a hill. Here in LA, a place like this would be worth millions. Master Harris turned to her and said with a wink, "Your safe word is apple."

She giggled, liking his sense of humor. He ushered her out of the car and into his home. Once they were inside, he walked her to a tiny room with a single chair.

"Sit and wait for your name to be called." He exited through a door on the other side. She could hear the clanging of metal instruments as he got things ready. She swallowed hard, her entire body a tangle of raw nerves.

The small waiting room was bland, with poor reproductions of classics hanging from the walls. There was even a side table with outdated magazines. All that was missing was some bad elevator music. This guy was really into the whole doctor routine. No wonder Lea had been thrilled by it—but it was totally lost on Brie.

She jumped when he opened the door. Her Dom

was dressed in a white coat, complete with a stethoscope hanging from his neck. "Hello, Miss Bennett. My name is Doctor Harris." He gave her a dimpled grin and held out his hand, his demeanor friendly and welcoming.

She slowly got up from the chair and shook his hand. He gave it a gentle squeeze and gestured for her to go into the room. As she walked by, he caressed the curve of her ass underneath her skirt. *Such a naughty doctor. Maybe this would be fun…*

The room was stark white with bright fluorescent lights overhead, and a patient table covered with disposable hygiene paper. She instantly noticed the change in temperature. Lea hadn't been kidding about the cold room. Brie's nipples hardened in protest.

She looked to the right and saw a silver tray with instruments laid out to be used on her. She quickly turned away when she noted the large syringe with a long, dangerous-looking needle. She suddenly felt a little faint, and gripped the edge of the table to keep her balance.

He began rattling off the familiar directions. "Please fully undress, including your bra and panties. A paper vest has been provided for you, but make sure it opens in the front. You can drape the second piece over your lap. I'll be back in a few minutes." He left her alone.

Brie felt momentarily paralyzed, terrified of what might happen to her under his care. She had to remind herself that she was there to live out her Dom's fantasy. She took a deep breath. *This isn't about my needs, this is about his.* Sir had assured them the Doms in these auctions had been fully screened and could be trusted. She had to accept that this man would stretch her in ways she wasn't prepared for, but would not hurt her. Well…there was a possibility he might try, but she would always have the safe word.

With his pleasure at the forefront of her mind, Brie donned her paper get-up and sat on the crinkly paper covering the exam table. She swung her feet absentmindedly while she watched her legs break out in goose bumps from the frigid air.

He entered with a smile and a wink. "Are we ready, Miss Bennett?"

"Yes, Doctor Harris."

"I'd prefer it if you'd just call me Doctor." He sat down on his stool and wheeled himself over to her. "So, why are you here today?"

Getting into her role, she answered, "Well, I haven't been to the doctor in a year. I assume I need a physical."

"I see… Have you had any health problems in the past?"

"No. Healthy as a horse."

He smiled charmingly. "Well, Miss Bennett, I'll still need to do a thorough exam to make sure you remain in good health." He tapped his hand on the table. "So why don't you lie down while I make this more comfy for you?" He pulled out the stirrups and gently placed her feet in each one. Playing the reluctant patient, Brie made sure her paper gown covered all the necessary parts as she repositioned herself.

He went straight for the good stuff. "When was the last time you did a manual breast exam?"

She bit her lip. "I don't remember."

He tsked. "You should be doing it every month, Miss

Bennett. You ought to be taking better care of yourself." He moved closer to her and slipped his hand under the paper vest. "You need to rub in a small, circular pattern all the way around your breast tissue." Doctor Harris stared into her eyes as he manipulated her breast. It was highly erotic, not at all like her normal breast exams.

After he had completely examined her left breast, he discreetly slipped his hand underneath the paper on the right side and started manipulating the other one. "You want to maintain the proper amount of pressure as you make your way around the entire breast area." His green eyes shone mischievously as he continued to touch her.

He pulled his hand out from under the vest when he was done. Brie was disappointed.

"I won't feel comfortable unless I'm assured you know how to do it yourself. I would like you to examine your left breast while I watch."

Brie felt a tingling in her groin as she pulled the paper away to expose her breast to him. She tentatively made circular motions at the top of her breast. His hand soon joined hers. "Like this, Miss Bennett." He guided her hand along as they both manipulated her bosom. When they made the final concentric circles over her areola, he bent over and she thought he was going to take her nipple into his mouth. Instead, he just breathed warm air on it. He looked at her and smiled. "I know this room is a tad cold."

She shuddered with need and frustration. He sat back down on his stool. "Now that we've established that you have good breast health, let's concentrate on the nether regions. When was the last time you had a pap?"

"A year ago. It's the reason I went to the doctor, actually."

"At least you are keeping up your vaginal health, but you are due for another." She heard the snap as he slipped on his rubber gloves. Then he picked up the metal speculum from the tray and scooted his chair between her legs.

"This is going to be chilly." He coated it with lubricant before easing the cold metal instrument into her vagina. Brie gasped at the temperature difference and her muscles clamped around the device.

"Relax, Miss Bennett. Remember, this is important for your health." He resumed his invasion and pushed the speculum deep inside her. "Now I am going to open it up, so I can have better access to you." She felt him twist it open, little by little, until the pressure inside became great. "That should about do it."

He grabbed one of the long swabs normally used for pap smears, but instead of jamming it up there to scrape off cervical cells, he caressed and teased her cervix with it. It caused a pleasurable ache she hadn't experienced before and she let out a small moan. He spent several minutes stroking her inside before he removed the swab and pulled out the speculum. Her Dom smiled between her legs. "Now that wasn't so bad, was it?"

She shook her head.

"Naturally, I need to manually examine your reproductive system. I'm sure you've experienced that before."

Brie had always hated that part of the examination, but something told her she might not mind it with Doctor Harris. He removed the paper covering without even asking, exposing her bare mound to his full gaze. Her Dom gave a low whistle. "I must say, Miss Bennett, you have an exceptionally beautiful vulva, and I've examined quite a few in my day."

Doctor Harris lathered his hands in lubricant and eased two fingers inside her. He pushed down on her belly and she could feel his hands caressing different organs. The way he did it, however, was sensual and not uncomfortable.

After he had finished, he stated, "A manual examination would not be complete without an anal examination as well." He lubed his fingers again and penetrated her ass with two fingers. She panted as he pushed his fingers deep inside. Again, he pressed against her stomach and massaged her internal organs. When he was done, however, his fingers remained in her ass.

"Your rectal muscles seem extremely tight. It's essential that you learn to relax them." With that, he started pumping his fingers inside her taut hole. "Focus on all those lovely nerve endings. Do you think you could take three fingers?"

Brie shook her head.

"I think you can." He inserted a third finger and stretched her ass wider. Brie squirmed, trying to avoid his invasion, but he pushed down on her stomach and effectively stopped her movements. "Stop moving and concentrate," he commanded. The true Dom was peeking through his friendly doctor persona.

Brie remained still, moaning as he fucked her ass with his fingers. "That's it. Relax, Miss Bennett." When her body stopped resisting his thrusts and opened up to him, he pulled his fingers out. The rubber gloves snapped as he removed them and tossed them into the trash.

"I was told that you trained in oral skills this week. Mind if I take a look at that mouth of yours?"

Brie shook her head.

He eyed her in amusement. "You don't speak much, do you?"

"Not to doctors," she said with a shy grin.

He snorted with laughter. "I would like to change that today." He moved to the end of the table and tilted her head back. "Let me take a good look inside there." He used a small flashlight and examined the back of her throat. "It looks a little red to me. Have you been engaging in deep-throat activities?"

"Yes, Doctor," she answered when he pulled away.

"It's irritating your throat. I would recommend you refrain from it for a couple of days. After today, of course."

"If it pleases you, Doctor," she answered.

"It does. Your overall health is my main concern, Miss Bennett."

"Yes, Doctor."

"I would like to perform a little-known procedure that aids in a woman's general health. You need to be naked for this. Please remove the vest." She sat up and slipped off the paper vest as he picked up a thin-looking phallus with a curve to it. Doctor Harris switched it on, and she could hear its rapid vibration. He turned it back off and asked with a grin, "Are you familiar with one of these?"

She shook her head, curious about its use.

He rubbed a small amount of lubricant over it, which automatically gave away its purpose. Brie tensed when he brought the device down between her legs. "They call this little beaut an anal stimulator. It's going to rock your world, Miss Bennett."

He slipped it inside and turned it on. Her whole body reverberated with the intense vibration. A gush of wetness dripped from her pussy.

"I see it is having the desired effect," he said with a wink. Her Dom unbuttoned his white coat, revealing a naked chest with well-defined biceps underneath. He removed his pants next, exposing his impressive cock, which stood erect and ready for action.

Doctor Harris smiled as he removed his stethoscope and laid it on the counter, leaving his coat on. Then he moved between her legs and stroked her inner thighs. "Such a lovely vulva deserves no less than my best care."

Brie wanted to continue playing the reluctant patient, so she whimpered, "Will it hurt?"

"Don't worry, Miss Bennett. This won't hurt a bit." He pressed the warm head of his cock against her opening and thrust in with one solid stroke.

Brie yelped. The anal stimulator made her tight and had her whole body buzzing. Her Dom cried out in pleasure as he slowly stroked her with his cock. Before long, however, he was thrusting with abandon.

She moaned and then cried, "No, Doctor, no! I can't take any more. Please stop!"

"It's important you lie still and take your treatment like a good patient." His thrusts became almost painful as he drove deep into her, hitting her cervix with every pass. She tried to arch her back for a different angle, but he held her stomach down and continued to fuck her hard.

The pressure he was applying did something to her. She felt her pussy start quivering as the ridge of his cock stimulated her engorged inner walls. What had started out as fake whimpers soon turned into screams of passion.

"You like the treatment, don't you?" he growled lustfully.

"God, yes, Doctor! I love it."

"To fully reap the benefit of my treatment, it is imperative that you orgasm. Think you can do that for me, Miss Bennett?"

She panted out ecstatically, "I'll…try…"

He pressed down even harder and ramped up his thrusting. She screamed in pleasure-pain as her body exploded in a powerful climax. He suddenly stopped to enjoy it. "That's it, milk your doctor's shaft." Her strong contractions squeezed his shaft shamelessly and continued far beyond what she was normally used to. By the time they had ended, she felt utterly undone.

He lifted his hands off her belly and slowly pulled out. However, he left the toy vibrating in her ass.

"Now that you are more relaxed, I think your body can handle more intense stimulation." He picked some small metal clamps up off the tray. "I have modified the springs so they won't cause any real damage, but they have a real bite to them. I won't lie to you, Miss Bennett. This *will* hurt a bit."

She flinched when he tried to touch her nipple.

"Movement is not allowed. I expect you to remain completely still as I apply this device to your nipple. Do you understand?"

Brie whispered in genuine fear, "Yes, Doctor."

"Look at me. Don't close your eyes or turn away." She watched as he pinched her nipple until it was perfectly erect. He reminded her again, "Don't move." The clamp closed down on her sensitive nipple and she squealed in pain, but did not twitch.

"Good," he said soothingly. A stray tear ran down her cheek as he prepared the second nipple. He looked directly into her eyes as he applied the second clamp. He smiled when she whimpered at the extreme pinch. "Your pupils are dilated right now. Those endorphins are kicking into overdrive." He kissed her then. She moaned when his tongue parted her lips and explored the contours of her mouth. "How I love a willing patient," he murmured.

He positioned her head so that it was slightly hanging off the edge of the table. "While you are adjusting to the new sensation, I want you to show off your newly acquired oral skills."

Brie gratefully grasped his cock, hoping it would distract her from her throbbing nipples. She ran her tongue over his head, paying special attention to the frenulum, the stringy part Mr. Gallant had taught her about.

He groaned appreciatively. "Nice."

While she stimulated him with her mouth, she caressed his balls with her hands. Then she moved southward and glided her finger over the soft skin between his cock and his anus. She started pressing against it and heard a rumble in his chest.

He squeezed the fullness of her breasts, which seemed to help ease the sharp pinch of the clamps. Brie could feel the pain slowly transforming into a dull, sensual ache. As it increased, the vibration in her ass began having a more positive effect. The combination of stimuli was mounting into another orgasm.

"Have you climaxed while deep-throating a man?" her Dom asked.

Brie disengaged from his cock. "No, Doctor."

"Excellent. I like to enjoy firsts with my patients." He placed his rigid member back in her mouth. "Keep the line of your throat straight for me." She fully expected that he would begin thrusting and she tensed, but he was slow and gentle, pressing the back of her throat, but then pulling back and pressing again a little harder. "Relax, Miss Bennett. This is an easy pill to swallow."

He sure had some cheesy doctor lines, but it was somewhat endearing. Brie obeyed him and opened her throat to his shaft. The head of his cock slid down halfway and then he stopped. After a few seconds, he pulled out so she could take a breath. "Well done. Let's try that again, but this time I want to add extra stimulation." He picked up the silver dildo from the tray. Brie snuck a quick peek and saw that only the giant syringe remained. She shuddered and looked back at the ceiling.

Her Dom smiled down at her. "Concentrate on your loins, Miss Bennett, while I enjoy that lusty throat of yours." He turned on the dildo to full vibration, which was in harmony with the one vibrating in her ass. She opened her mouth to him and he inserted his cock, pushing past the resistance and deep into her throat.

He leaned over, positioning the vibrator against her needy clit. She twitched when it made contact and moaned softly, but the sound of her pleasure was muffled by his large cock. He moved the dildo over her clit slowly, teasingly.

Just as the blood started pounding in her head, he pulled out so she could catch a breath. "I enjoy the control you have over your throat," he complimented. "I have a better understanding of why you received a seven for your first auction."

It was news to Brie that the bidding Doms had been informed of their prior ratings. It explained the lack of enthusiasm at Mary's auction. She couldn't help wondering how this Dom would rate her, but those thoughts flew out of the window when his dick claimed her throat again.

He pressed the vibrator hard against her clit as he pushed deep into her. The buildup was rushing forward to a crescendo she couldn't control. She almost gave in to it, but he pulled back and said soothingly, "Not yet, Miss Bennett. Not yet."

Her body was a torrent of sensation from the harmonic vibrations of the toys, the dull, throbbing ache of the clamps, and the total feeling of possession as he forced his cock down her throat. She was willingly and completely at his mercy.

He played with her breasts again, tugging lightly on the clamps, making her instantly aware again of their painful bite. "Now we're ready. Take several deep breaths. I want to savor it."

She breathed in deeply, infusing her blood with oxygen, before opening her mouth to him. He slid his cock into her throat, deeper than before, and then pressed the vibrator against the side of her erect clit. Her whole body tensed as it readied itself for release.

"Concentrate on all the sensations, Miss Bennett. Live in the moment and succumb to them."

Brie didn't last long, her body desperate for the impending orgasm. Her pelvis lifted off the paper, her heart beating like a drum as the first contraction hit. She made guttural noises as her ass muscles clamped around the anal stimulator and her clit pulsed in time with it. His cock became still, deep in her throat, and then began its own pulsing rhythm. They were in sync as they climaxed together. Hers ended before his and she had to lie quietly, not allowing herself to panic as he finished his orgasm.

He slowly pulled out and then stroked her face as he leaned over to kiss her forehead. "Now, remember what I said. No more cocks down your throat for at least two days. Doctor's orders."

She stared up at him and smiled. He really did have an odd sense of humor she enjoyed.

That happy feeling disappeared when he went for the last item on the tray. He held up the large syringe and pushed on the plunger. Clear liquid dripped down the length of the needle. Her eyes widened in fear.

He looked down at her and grinned. "I put this out solely for your benefit, Miss Bennett. I assumed a woman afraid of doctors must be afraid of needles. It is simply a prop."

Brie started giggling out of relief. The laughter soon became uncontrollable as tears ran down her face.

His green eyes sparkled with amusement. "I had you going, didn't I?"

She nodded vigorously, unable to speak. She went to wipe the wetness from her eyes, but he stopped her.

Her Dom leaned down and kissed her tears away. "Nothing is as sweet as tears of laughter, Miss Bennett."

Doctor Harris helped her with her clothes before he dressed himself. Then he surprised her by taking her out to a small but exclusive restaurant. Instead of spending the entire time fucking her, this Dom chose to make conversation over plates of Portobello ravioli and red wine. He asked about her film experience and didn't laugh when she told him about her film shorts. He seemed genuinely interested in her beyond her submissive persona, and it impressed Brie.

As she watched him over dinner, however, Brie realized that Doctor Harris didn't have a chance with her. Yes, he was witty and charming, but he lacked Sir's intense stare and the slight smirk that made her want to quiver at his feet. She was excited when the time came to return to the Center.

Once again, the three girls detailed their experiences for the panel. During the debriefing, Brie found out that Lea had spent the day acting out the role of a private to a very demanding female sergeant, while Mary had played the reluctant hooker being wooed by a smooth-talking pimp. Brie was relieved that Mary had had a positive experience this time around—it had made the normally unpleasant woman much more animated and personable.

After Sir had dismissed them, Brie invited Lea to join her after class for a little female debriefing and drinks. Mary remained in her seat, checking through her purse for something. Just as the elevator doors began to close, Brie felt a twinge of guilt. She stuck her arm out to open the doors back up.

"Hey, Mary Quite Contrary, you wanna hang for a bit?" Mary glared at her with her chin in the air, but Brie wasn't fooled by her act. "Seriously, Lea and I want you to come. It'll be fun."

"Fine. Whatever." Mary gathered her things and joined them in the elevator.

Lea looked at Brie questioningly, and then turned to Mary. "I hope you're planning to buy several rounds of drinks. It's the only way I'll be able to stand you."

Brie was surprised by Lea's honesty, and stood there wondering how Mary would react.

"I insist," Mary said with a smile. "With a couple of rum and Cokes in my bloodstream you might actually start to sound intelligent."

Lea stuck out her tongue.

Brie couldn't help it. She started to giggle and then it dissolved into uncontrolled laughter. Lea soon joined her. Brie watched Mary's expression twitch, then crumble, and then she began laughing, too.

In that moment, the three became a true sisterhood. Brie beamed at the other two. *Look at us—the Three Musketeers of Submission.* The Training Center had no idea what it was in for...

What kind of trouble can these three get into?
Find out in *Love Me*.

Buy the next in the series:

#1   #2   #3

Brie's Submission in order:

Teach Me #1
Love Me #2
Catch Me #3
Try Me #4
Protect Me #5
Hold Me #6
Surprise Me #7
Trust Me #8
Claim Me #9

You can find Red on:
Twitter: @redphoenix69
Website: RedPhoenix69.com
Facebook: RedPhoenix69

**Keep up to date with the newest release of Brie by signing up for Red Phoenix's newsletter:
redphoenix69.com/newsletter-signup**

Red Phoenix is the author of:

Blissfully Undone
* Available in eBook and paperback
(Snowy Fun—Two people find themselves snowbound in a cabin where hidden love can flourish, taking one couple on a sensual journey into ménage à trois)

His Scottish Pet: Dom of the Ages
* Available in eBook and paperback
Audio Book: *His Scottish Pet: Dom of the Ages*
(Scottish Dom—A sexy Dom escapes to Scotland in the late 1400s. He encounters a waif who has the potential to free him from his tragic curse)

The Erotic Love Story of Amy and Troy
* Available in eBook and paperback
(Sexual Adventures—True love reigns, but fate continually throws Troy and Amy into the arms of others)

eBooks

Varick: The Reckoning

(Savory Vampire—A dark, sexy vampire story. The hero
navigates the dangerous world he has been thrust into
with lusty passion and a pure heart)

Keeper of the Wolf Clan (Keeper of Wolves, #1)

(Sexual Secrets—A virginal werewolf must act as the
clan's mysterious Keeper)

The Keeper Finds Her Mate (Keeper of Wolves, #2)

(Second Chances—A young she-wolf must choose
between old ties or new beginnings)

The Keeper Unites the Alphas (Keeper of Wolves, #3)

(Serious Consequences—The young she-wolf is captured
by the rival clan)

Boxed Set: Keeper of Wolves Series (Books 1-3)

(Surprising Secrets—A secret so shocking it will rock
Layla's world. The young she-wolf is put in a position of
being able to save her werewolf clan or becoming the
reason for its destruction)

Socrates Inspires Cherry to Blossom

(Satisfying Surrender—a mature and curvaceous woman becomes fascinated by an online Dom who has much to teach her)

By the Light of the Scottish Moon

(Saving Love—Two lost souls, the Moon, a werewolf and a death wish…)

In 9 Days

(Sweet Romance—A young girl falls in love with the new student, nicknamed 'the Freak')

---

9 Days and Counting

(Sacrificial Love—The sequel to In 9 Days delves into the emotional reunion of two longtime lovers)

And Then He Saved Me

(Saving Tenderness—When a young girl tries to kill herself, a man of great character intervenes with a love that heals)

Play With Me at Noon

(Seeking Fulfillment—A desperate wife lives out her fantasies by taking five different men in five days)

Connect with Red on Substance B

Substance B is a new platform for independent authors to directly connect with their readers. Please visit Red's Substance B page where you can:

- Sign up for Red's newsletter
- Send a message to Red
- See all platforms where Red's books are sold

Visit Substance B today to learn more about your favorite independent authors.

Made in the USA
San Bernardino, CA
30 March 2017